Playground Plague

JAKE LANCING

PUFFIN

With special thanks to David J. Gatward

PUFFIN BOOKS

Published by the Penguin Group
Penguin Books Ltd, 80 Strand, London WC2R ORL, England
Penguin Group (USA) Inc., 375 Hudson Street, New York, New York 10014, USA
Penguin Group (Canada), 90 Eglinton Avenue East, Suite 700, Toronto, Ontario, Canada M4P 2Y3
(a division of Pearson Penguin Canada Inc.)
Penguin Ireland, 25 St Stephen's Green, Dublin 2, Ireland (a division of Penguin Books Ltd)
Penguin Group (Australia), 250 Camberwell Road, Camberwell, Victoria 3124, Australia
(a division of Pearson Australia Group Pty Ltd)
Penguin Books India Pvt Ltd, 11 Community Centre, Panchsheel Park, New Delhi – 110 017, India
Penguin Group (NZ), 67 Apollo Drive, Rosedale, North Shore 0632, New Zealand
(a division of Pearson New Zealand Ltd)
Penguin Books (South Africa) (Pty) Ltd, 24 Sturdee Avenue, Rosebank,
Johannesburg 2196, South Africa

Penguin Books Ltd, Registered Offices: 80 Strand, London WC2R ORL, England

puffinbooks.com

First published 2010
1

Text copyright © Hothouse Fiction Ltd, 2010
All rights reserved

Set in Bembo Book MT 13.5/19.25 pt
Typeset by Palimpsest Book Production Limited, Grangemouth, Stirlingshire
Made and printed in England by Clays Ltd, St Ives plc

British Library Cataloguing in Publication Data
A CIP catalogue record for this book is available from the British Library

ISBN: 978-0-141-32461-6

www.greenpenguin.co.uk

Playground Plague

Jake Lancing lives in Somerset. When not writing about adventure-seeking, football-playing angels, he spends his time avoiding work, listening to very uncool music, growing his hair, and helping the government to catch spies.★ He jumped out of a plane once because it seemed like a good idea at the time.

★ One of those things might not be *entirely* true.

Books by Jake Lancing

DEMON DEFENDERS:
CLASSROOM DEMONS

DEMON DEFENDERS:
ZOMBIES IN THE HOUSE

DEMON DEFENDERS:
GOBLIN GAMES

DEMON DEFENDERS:
PLAYGROUND PLAGUE

For George

Contents

1
Bottling It

'Oi!' cried Spit. 'Watch where you're waving that spanner!'

It was Saturday afternoon, and Alex, Cherry, Spit, Inchy and Big House were crowded into the dusty attic above number 92 Eccles Road. The room had been small enough to begin with, but with most of the available space taken up by large wooden packing cases and five young angels crammed in too, there wasn't enough room to swing a cat.

In the middle of the floor, Alex had laid out a

large sheet of paper with a complicated-looking diagram on it. It looked like assembly instructions for a space shuttle. On top of the sheet stood a tall, almost-completed set of shelves.

'There!' panted Alex, screwing the last shelf into place. 'Finished!'

He looked around at the others. They were all dusty, grimy and red in the face. Cherry had a large cobweb dangling from the peak of her baseball cap and Inchy had a cockroach nesting in his hair. The instructions had promised that it would take twenty-five minutes to put the shelves together. The gang had been working on them for five hours.

'Wonderful,' muttered Spit. 'Now all we have to do is bolt them to the wall. That should only take another week or so.'

'Pants to that,' replied Alex. 'We need to get this job finished quickly.'

'Agreed,' said Cherry. 'We've got some serious footie practice to get in. We don't want to look like idiots when we get back to school after the holidays.'

'Well you won't,' said Spit, 'just so long as you don't go wearing *that*.'

Cherry, dressed in her favourite stripy leggings, army jacket and biker boots, glared at him. Inchy jumped in before another fashion row could erupt.

'But Tabbris told us we have to get these shelves up before we can do anything else,' he said. 'He wants them to store his collection of vintage lemonades.'

'Just out of interest,' said House, easing his big frame down on to one of the packing cases filled with dusty bottles, 'what kind of nugget *stores* lemonade? I mean, lemonade's for drinking, isn't it?'

Spit flicked his black hair out of his eyes, a well practised look of disdain on his face. 'I'd say this is one of his more normal interests.'

As well as being obsessively neat and tidy, the whole gang knew that their guardian, the retired Special Operations angel Major Tabbris, had a number of strange hobbies – from clipping his garden hedges into the shape of armoured tanks, to collecting porcelain pigs.

House grinned and pulled a sandwich out of his pocket. Bigger and stronger than the rest of the gang, he needed food. And lots of it. Lunch had been a whole hour ago – he was starving.

'So how are we going to get this job finished, then,' he mumbled, spraying crumbs everywhere.

A confident smile slipped across Alex's face.

'Oh no,' said Cherry.

Everyone knew what Alex was going to say next.

'I have a plan.'

There was a low groan from the group. They were well aware that all Alex's plans should come with a warning – *May Go Badly Wrong*.

'Don't worry,' said Alex. 'This one's pure genius.'

'Rope?' said Spit, as Alex picked up a dusty coil from the top of one of the packing cases. 'That's your plan?'

Alex nodded, smiling.

'Yeah – there's no need to spend hours bolting the shelves to the wall. If we just tie them to that water pipe there, we'll be finished in half an hour, max!'

'Are you sure,' said Cherry, looking at the rusty pipe that ran along one wall of the attic. 'It doesn't look very strong.'

'It's made of metal, isn't it?' replied Alex. 'It'll be fine. Tabbris won't care how we get the shelves to stand up. All he wants is his precious and unnecessarily weird lemonade stored safely. And it will be. OK?'

'I suppose it might work,' said Inchy.

'It's not as bad as some of your other plans,' admitted Spit grudgingly.

'Good,' said Alex. 'Let's get to it!'

The gang leapt into action and twenty minutes later the job was done.

'Bomb proof,' said Alex, reaching up to put the last of Tabbris's 348 lemonade bottles in place.

'Maybe,' said Inchy. 'Are you sure those knots will hold?'

'My knots always hold,' said Alex, staring at their handiwork.

The shelves certainly looked safe, securely tied to the pipe by numerous bits of rope. Alex gave them a tug.

'No movement,' he said. 'Job done!'

'I can't quite believe it,' said Cherry.

'Glad you've got so much confidence in me,' replied Alex.

'Oh, I think she's got more than enough confidence in you,' said Spit. 'Like the rest of us, she's completely confident in your ability to mess things up.'

'Not this time, though,' Alex smirked. 'Now, who's for a bit of footie?'

The gang erupted in a chorus of cheers.

With just a hint of a swagger, Alex led the way towards the trapdoor that led back downstairs. Suddenly, Inchy stopped.

'Erm, what was that?' he asked nervously.

'What was what?'

A soft groan echoed through the attic.

'*That.*'

The gang stopped and listened. The groan came again, louder this time.

'I may not be an expert on human buildings,' said Spit, 'but I'm pretty sure that creaking noises in a loft are *not* a good sign.'

The creaking sound came again, even louder.

'Right, no one move!' ordered Alex.

'No one *is* moving,' snapped Cherry.

For a few seconds, everyone held their breath. Dust danced in the fingers of sunlight that poked their way through gaps in the roof. Outside, a bored pigeon cooed.

Alex breathed out.

'I think it's OK,' he said, taking another step towards the trapdoor.

Which was when the pipe broke.

With a thunderous crash, the lemonade shelf collapsed, sending bottles flying in all directions. Water spewed from the broken pipe as if from a fireman's hose. Within seconds, the floor was awash.

Alex splashed over to the pipe and tried desperately to plug it, but the gushing water was too strong and pushed his hands away.

'Come on, you lot! Help!'

The rest of the gang tried to run across to him, but instead they had to wade, the water was already so deep.

'We can't stop it!' cried Spit.

'We can!' spluttered Alex. 'Just block the pipe!'

'With what exactly?' yelled Cherry, over the roar of water. 'Your cotton wool brain?!'

Before Alex could reply, a new, louder groaning noise sounded from beneath his feet. He had just enough time to say 'Uh-oh' before the floor gave way and the gang yelled as they disappeared straight down the hole.

Alex landed with a thump on the bathroom floor, hotly pursued by about a hundred litres of water. Spit and Cherry ended up head first in the laundry basket, Inchy's bum was wedged firmly into the sink, and House bellyflopped into the bathtub.

Silence fell as Alex surveyed the destruction. Nobody seemed to have hurt themselves. For a moment, he felt a flood of relief. Then, as the dust settled, he saw a dreadfully familiar figure sitting upright in the bath. Too tall and thin to be House, the figure might have been wearing soap suds and a shower cap rather than a tweed suit, and clutching a loofah rather than its usual cane, but there was no mistaking who it was . . .

With a bubbling gurgle, House burst to the surface of the bath and found himself staring right into the face of Major Tabbris, Order of Raphael, 1st Class.

House coughed. 'We're in big, big trouble.'

'So much for your great and tremendous plan to get outside and enjoy a bit of footie in the sunshine,' snarled Spit.

'Shut up and keep peeling,' said House.

Alex looked at Spit, then at the rest of the gang, then at the enormous sack of potatoes that stood next to them.

'Look –' he began.

'Don't!' said Cherry, without even looking up. 'Don't say a word.'

'But –'

'I agree with Cherry on this one,' snapped Spit. 'And I never agree with Cherry on anything.'

'But I'm sorry.'

'Heard it before,' said Inchy, grabbing another potato and wiping his brow.

'We'll have plenty of time to play footie anyway,' said Alex. 'There's another five-a-side competition at school this term.'

'Yeah, because we did so well in the last one,' said House sarcastically.

'That wasn't my fault!' protested Alex.

'Ah,' said a deep voice from the doorway. 'I wondered how long it would be before you tried that particular excuse.'

Alex's heart sank as Tabbris limped across the

room, his cane tapping. With a grunt, he bent over and picked up a peeled potato from the small pile in the centre of the gang. He stared at it for a moment, then held it up close to Alex's nose.

'Does this look peeled to you?'

Alex stared at the potato, going slightly cross-eyed in the process.

'Er, yeah.'

'And that lack of judgement is why you so often find yourself in trouble,' replied Tabbris. 'Take this potato . . .'

'Where?' asked House.

Tabbris frowned and House shut up.

'You think that this potato is peeled,' continued Tabbris. 'All skin perfectly removed. A shining example of the skill of peeling. One you could use at a world potato-peeling fair to demonstrate the art of peeling in all its finery, yes?'

No one really knew what Tabbris was on about, so they just nodded.

'But alas,' said Tabbris, pointing at the potato. 'It is not. See?'

The gang leaned in.

'A speck of skin,' barked Tabbris, his moustache bristling. 'Not much to you, perhaps, but something you missed. Something someone else will have to sort out, because you didn't do the job properly.'

Tabbris handed the potato to House.

'Think about it, please,' he said crisply, turning to leave. 'If you want to get back to Heaven, then stop missing the specks, stop cutting corners, and stop leaving a trail of destruction in your wake. Or you'll find yourselves staying here forever. And I am sure that is the last thing *any* of us want.'

No one argued.

And with that, Tabbris was gone.

House stared at the potato. 'Mental,' he said.

'Not as mental as us having Alex as leader,' muttered Cherry.

'Hang on,' said Alex. 'I know stuff's gone wrong now and again, but –'

'"Now and again"?' spluttered Spit. 'Presumably by that you mean "all the time"?'

'What about everything that's gone *right*?' said Alex. 'We've saved Green Hill from zombies, demons and even goblins!'

'Yes,' said Spit, 'but we're still trapped on Earth, aren't we? So it hasn't done us any good at all.'

'We never get a good report back to Cloud Nine Academy,' agreed Inchy.

'And we keep getting these horrible punishments from Tabbris,' added Cherry.

'Which really sucks,' finished House.

Alex couldn't believe what he was hearing. 'So you think I'm rubbish, is that it?' he demanded.

There was a long silence. None of the gang would meet Alex's eye. Even House looked away.

'Fine,' said Alex huffily. 'If one of you thinks you can do a better job as leader, just say so.'

'I do say so,' said Spit. 'Anyone would be better than you.'

'Right, well you have a go, then!' shouted Alex angrily. 'I quit! As of now, Spit's in charge!'

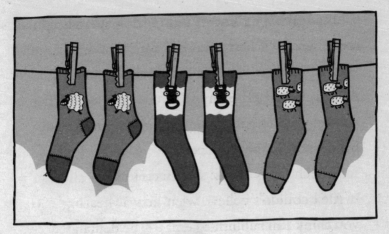

2
Furry Friends

'Cherry, that's not a good idea.'

Cherry froze, her hand stuck in mid-air as she reached for the washing line. She looked round guiltily.

'Says who?'

'Says me. And I'm the new team captain, remember?'

Cherry stared at Spit, then back to the washing line. Tabbris's socks – woolly green ones covered in inexplicably awful pictures of fluffy sheep – were within reach. Her fingers twitched. It was a bright morning, but Cherry was in a dark mood, and she wanted revenge, no matter how small.

'But he deserves it,' she complained. 'That potato-peeling punishment was totally unfair. My hands are still wrinkled from the water. So Tabbris's socks are going to pay a little visit to Mr Blender in the kitchen.'

Cherry reached out again.

'Cherry . . .'

Her hand slipped round a sock.

'Cherry!'

'What?'

'It's not worth it,' said Spit. 'Tabbris is an old grump, but getting our own back will only make him worse.'

'But —' said Cherry.

'No "buts",' said Spit. 'If we don't get *into* trouble, Tabbris won't *be* any trouble. It's that simple.'

'If you believe that, you'll believe anything,' grumbled Alex, stepping out from behind Spit.

Spit turned to him, his face serious. 'I'm just trying to speed up our return to Heaven, that's all.

Isn't that what the leader is supposed to do?' He smiled smugly.

With a sigh, Cherry stuffed her hands into her pockets and backed away from the washing line to join the rest of the gang, scuffing her shoes along the ground.

'All right, we'll try it your way,' she said, swinging her school bag on to her shoulder. 'But I still think he deserves it.'

Spit looked hard at Alex. 'See?'

'See what, exactly?' said Alex. 'A spoilsport killjoy who wouldn't recognize fun if it bit him on his bony bum?'

'No,' said Spit. 'A bit of responsibility. That's the key to real leadership.'

'The key to total boredom, more like,' muttered Alex under his breath as the gang slouched out through the gate. 'This is going to be really hard . . .'

By the time the gang arrived at school, Alex had changed his mind. Having Spit as leader wasn't going to be hard, it was going to be *impossible*. He had stopped Alex from doing anything mischievous at all on the journey – even something completely harmless, like sticking a couple of peeled potatoes in the exhaust pipe of the headmaster's car.

The rest of the gang had been equally surprised at how strict he was. After all, Spit had never shown much desire to be in charge before. Making jokes and having a laugh from the sidelines was more his style. But they all knew how desperate he was to get back to Heaven. Maybe when you wanted something that badly, you would do anything to get it.

Now the gang were in their first lesson of the day (science – *boooooooring*), waiting for the teacher to arrive. Alex and House were sitting together, with Inchy and Cherry next to them, and Spit on his own behind them. It felt to Alex like he was sitting there to keep an eye on them all. The worst thing was, none of the others seemed to mind. In fact, House seemed positively thrilled.

'I can't believe we got all the way to school without getting into trouble once,' he gushed. 'That's a first. Nobody shouted at us or anything.'

'Yeah. Great,' said Alex glumly, folding his arms

and slumping down in his chair. Even his best mate was on Spit's side. Unbelievable.

'Don't be like that,' House smiled. 'We're all in this together. And we all want to get back to Heaven. Right?'

'And you think Spit's the one to get us there, do you?'

House opened his mouth to say something, but was interrupted by the classroom door, which burst open with a bang. Standing in the doorway was a twitchy little man with a straggly moustache, struggling to keep hold of a stack of cloth-covered boxes. His worn, brown corduroy suit made him look like a small, skinny bar of chocolate.

'Mr Roddan has all the best outfits,' giggled House as the teacher staggered to the front of the classroom. 'Think I might get one.'

'Yeah, brown is really your colour,' said Alex. 'What do you think he's got in those boxes?'

House squinted. 'Whatever it is, it doesn't seem too happy about it.'

House was right. As Mr Roddan struggled past

the gang, an irritable squeak sounded from under one of the covers.

'Weird,' said Inchy. 'What could it be?'

'I think we're about to find out,' replied Spit as, after much grunting and groaning, Mr Roddan finally managed to get the pile of boxes on to his desk.

'I've never liked his moustache,' whispered Cherry as Mr Roddan puffed himself up to speak. 'It looks like a furry caterpillar just crawled on to his top lip. And died.'

House managed to muffle his laugh as Mr Roddan opened his mouth to address them.

'Good morning, students!' he said, his voice squeaking like a badly oiled door. 'Say hello to your new classmates!'

With a theatrical flourish, he pulled the cover off one of the boxes.

'That's not a box,' said House, 'it's a cage.'

'And what's that inside?' Cherry craned her neck for a better view, along with the rest of the class.

At first, they couldn't see anything apart from a large pile of wood shavings. Then, a small shape emerged. Black and furry, with a pointed nose, whiskers and a long, worm-like tail.

'Is that what I think it is?' asked Alex disbelievingly.

Mr Roddan beamed a cat-that's-got-the-cream smile. 'Indeed it is. A rat!'

Someone screamed. Someone else jumped up on to their chair. One girl near the front actually ran out of the room.

'Your new science project!' said Mr Roddan, utterly oblivious to the current of horror sweeping its way round the class.

'From today,' he continued, 'you will all be responsible for these delightful, fascinating creatures. And by responsible, I mean feeding! Cleaning! Talking to them! Making sure they're comfy!'

The shock wave took itself on another circuit of the classroom.

'At the same time, you will establish,' continued Mr Roddan, bouncing up and down on his toes and clapping his hands with glee, 'through careful tests and observations, which type of food is preferred by the humble rat: peanuts, cheese or chocolate drops!'

'He's a bit overexcited, isn't he?' muttered House.

'You know what teachers are like,' replied Alex. 'They always think their lessons are brilliant, even when they're pants.'

'Come!' said Mr Roddan, beckoning to the class. 'Your work groups are the same as last term. I have provided one rat for each group. Come! And let science be your guide!'

Cherry climbed out of her seat, marched smartly up to the front of the room and returned with a cage.

'Here we are,' she announced. 'Our rat.'

The gang stared at the rodent inside the cage. It was brown, with a distinctive white patch over one eye. For a moment, the rat stared back with bright black eyes. Then it scampered over to the corner of the cage, lay down on a pile of wood shavings and went to sleep.

'Charming,' said Cherry.

'Being a rat must be ace,' said House. 'I mean, all you do is eat and sleep. How cool is that?'

Alex frowned. 'Not really fair, though, is it? To be locked up in a cage and experimented on.'

'Yeah, but all that free food,' sighed House. 'Bliss.'

Cherry shuffled round to have a closer look. 'It's a stupid experiment anyway,' she said. 'It's bound to choose the chocolate, isn't it?'

'You're a bit quiet, Inch,' said Alex, turning to his small friend. 'Oh!'

Inchy's face was grey. His eyes were bulging. His fingers gripped the tabletop so hard that it looked like they might leave dents in the surface, and he was quivering like a jelly in a tumble dryer.

'What's the matter, Inchy?' asked House, worried.

'I don't really like rats.' Inchy's voice was a whisper.

'But there's nothing to be scared of,' said Cherry. 'They're quite cute, really.'

'I know it's irrational,' admitted Inchy, shivering. 'But I just can't bear them. They always look like they're plotting something, or that they've been talking about you behind your back.'

'Maybe it would help if we gave our rat a name,' suggested Alex. 'To make him seem more like a person.'

'Don't be daft,' said Spit.

'I'm not,' protested Alex. 'I think he looks like a Gerald.'

21

'What do you think, Inchy?' said Cherry with an encouraging smile.

'I think he looks like a rat.'

Spit sighed. 'This is going to be a long term . . .'

On the way home, the gang stopped off at the park to have a kick around, using their school bags as makeshift goalposts. Spit took charge, immediately arranging teams differently to how Alex normally did it. He put House with Inchy, Cherry with Alex, and made himself referee. It was two-a-side, rush goalie and first to three goals.

Inchy scored first, after a stunning cross by House over Cherry's head. Alex scored the equalizer, slipping it between House's legs as he went for the save. Then Cherry scored again with a nifty little header that made Spit cheer. Finally, House came back, not just with an equalizer that he chipped past a diving Alex, but a fantastic winner, slammed in from his own goal.

'Well done, guys,' beamed Spit as the team scooped up their bags. 'That was a great practice. It's already given me some new ideas for our first match. With me in charge, perhaps we've got a chance this season.'

Alex looked over at his new captain darkly. He had to admit, it *had* been a good practice. The best they'd had for weeks, in fact. But that didn't stop Alex spending the rest of the walk home secretly wishing that Spit would trip up over his own ego.

3
A New Leaf

'So just let me make sure I've got this quite clear,'
said Alex, disbelief carved on to his face. 'You want
us to make *Tabbris* a *afternoon tea.*'

The way he emphasized the words left nobody
in any doubt as to what he thought of the idea.

The gang were sitting in the shed that hid at the
very back of Tabbris's exceptionally neat and well-
groomed garden. Spit was standing in front of the
gang. Behind him, nailed to the wall, was a large
sheet of paper with the words *RETURN TO*

HEAVEN – CAMPAIGN PLAN written on it in big red letters.

Alex hadn't been able to force himself to read any further than the first point: *Make Tabbris afternoon tea*.

'Do you have a problem with that, Alex?' said Spit reasonably. 'Because now is the time to speak up.'

'No, not at all,' said Alex, shuffling on the upturned wooden crate he was using as a seat. 'No complaining from me. After all, providing afternoon tea is *exactly* what we angels are trained for, isn't it?'

Inchy opened his mouth to say something, but then saw the look on Alex's face, and decided to keep very quiet instead.

'Oh yes,' Alex continued. 'Baking buns, serving piping hot Earl Grey tea, putting pointless paper doilies on plates. It all says *angel* better than banishing demons or destroying zombies, I'd say.'

'Look –' said Spit, but Alex was on a roll.

'You know what,' he continued, 'I reckon when we get back to Heaven, Gabriel won't be able to *wait* to start using your ideas. What's next? Advanced classes in ironing skills and needlework? Ten ways to use a mop to help humanity?'

House ignored the argument, leaned forward, and took a biscuit. Then thought about it again and took three more. The plate was almost empty and soon would be if he had anything to do with it. The oat crumblies he'd picked up from old Mrs Kowalski the day before were totally delicious. Ever since the gang had helped save her husband from the zombies infesting Green Hill Hospital, she'd provided them with delicious, home-made biscuits every week. Not that anyone other than House ever really got to eat any. And not one of them knew about the other things she baked that had never quite made it all the way home . . .

'Finished?' said Cherry, looking at Alex.

Alex opened his mouth again.

'Good,' said Cherry, cutting him off. 'Because whether you like it or not, we're going to give Spit's ideas a chance.'

'But —'

'And if that means I have to make a few sandwiches,' said Cherry, her ponytail bouncing, 'or pour a cup of tea or two for old Tabbris, then that's fine by me. I want to get back to Heaven. End of.'

'Fine!' said Alex, folding his arms huffily.

The gang looked back at Spit.

'Thank you, Cherry,' he said. 'OK, to make this easier, I've given us all specific jobs to do. That way we can be sure everything's been done and nothing should go wrong.'

'Yeah, right,' murmured Alex. 'Where have I heard *that* one before . . .'

'So how do I use this, then?' asked Cherry.

In her hand was a tall metal rod, the end of which was attached to a small, rectangular metal box. Sticking out of the bottom of the box were some rollers covered in bristles.

'It's a cleaner,' explained Inchy. 'You just sort of push it.'

'But I thought vacuum cleaners had to be plugged in?' said Cherry. 'Where's the cable?'

'Doesn't have one,' said Inchy. 'It's a mechanical sweeper. Pretty old. I don't think Tabbris has even *heard* of vacuum cleaners.'

Cherry pushed the thing forward. It made a sort of *ruh-da-da-da-da* sound and a small cloud of fluff rose from the carpet.

'You'll probably need to push it a bit quicker than that,' said Inchy. 'Or it won't pick anything up, but just spread it all around a bit.'

'I'm glad I'm only doing in here,' said Cherry, looking round the living room. 'It's still going to take ages, though.'

'Well, you've only got twenty minutes,' said Inchy. 'Everything has to be ready for when Tabbris is back from his walk in the park.'

Cherry shook her head. 'Can you believe we're doing this?'

Inchy looked at Cherry, but said nothing.

'Didn't think so.'

A frustrated yowl echoed down the hall.

'That's House,' explained Inchy. 'He's polishing the silver. He's already bent three spoons.'

Cherry let out a faint laugh. 'How's your harp playing coming along?'

Inchy had been given the job of playing relaxing music to Tabbris while he ate.

He shrugged. 'I'm a bit out of practice. Put it this way – we can only hope Tabbris is as deaf as he seems to be.'

Spit's head appeared round the living-room door. 'It's exactly T minus seventeen minutes. We haven't got time for dilly-dallying,' he said. Then he was gone again.

'He said "dilly-dallying",' said Cherry.

And they both roared with laughter.

'I hate cooking,' grumbled Alex to no one in particular. He'd been given the job of making the scones and sorting out the pot of tea. 'I hate kitchens and weighing scales and flour and eggs. I hate ovens and butter and greaseproof paper. I hate –'

'Er, Alex?'

Alex turned. House was standing in the kitchen doorway, holding a knife that looked more like a boomerang.

'Can't you bend it back?' said Alex.

'It *is* bent back,' sighed House. 'But it still looks wonky. Of all the jobs Spit could've given me . . .'

'You mean polishing cutlery isn't in your

Guardian Angel Handbook?' Alex grinned. 'Is there not a section on being a butler?'

'Ha ha,' said House. 'How are the scones?'

Alex's smile transformed into a frown.

'Let's just say my second batch needs to be better than the first,' he said, picking up what appeared to be a small black rock from a plate in the middle of the kitchen table.

'Oh,' said House. 'How did you do that?'

'I don't know,' said Alex. He picked up a fresh tray of uncooked scones and opened the oven. 'I just hope these turn out better. Spit will never let me hear the end of it otherwise.'

Just as Alex pushed the oven door shut, Spit himself appeared. House hid the bent knife behind his back. Alex stood in front of the table to conceal the burnt scones.

'Gentlemen,' said Spit, horribly serious and stern. 'We have ten minutes.'

'No problem,' said House and Alex together, forcing smiles.

'Really,' added Alex. 'Everything's fine and dandy.'

Spit looked at them both. 'It had better be. If we

get this right, we could be on our way back to Heaven before the week is out . . .'

Tabbris reached for another scone.

'Allow me, sir!'

Spit reached over, buttered a scone, spread it with a thick layer of rich clotted cream, dolloped on some strawberry jam, and handed it to Tabbris.

'More tea, sir?'

'Yes, that would be most agreeable, Respite,' said Tabbris. Alex grinned to see a bit of the old Spit reappear as the young angel winced slightly at the sound of his full name.

Tabbris was sitting in his favourite armchair, which had been pulled up close to a merrily crackling fire. Soothing music came from the corner, where Inchy sat over his harp, frowning with concentration. Spit, wearing a black jacket and bow tie, stood at Tabbris's elbow, while the rest of the gang sat awkwardly on the sofa, dressed in the smartest clothes they had been able to find. In Alex's case, this was a blazer and straw hat, for House a waistcoat that was at least three sizes too small for him, and for Cherry a full length evening dress and blonde wig. Alex didn't know whether to laugh or cry. On the one hand, he felt like a total idiot. On the other, he grudgingly admitted, the afternoon tea seemed to be going rather well.

Tabbris sipped his tea and took a bite of his scone.

'Delicious,' he said, carefully brushing crumbs from his moustache.

'Thank you, sir,' murmured Spit. 'This is just our way of saying sorry for the accident in the attic, and thank you for looking after us so well since we've been here. We really do appreciate it.'

In the corner, Inchy sighed silently. He'd already got to the end of the three songs he could remember from Cloud Nine Academy and was now just repeating himself, adding in the occasional improvised tune that didn't always work.

Tabbris finished his scone, sat back in his chair, and looked at the gang.

'Are there any scones left?'

Alex nodded. Despite the first batch being a total disaster, the second had come out brilliantly.

'Good,' said Tabbris. 'Then why don't you go

and fetch some, so we can all enjoy them together? I think that would be rather jolly, don't you?'

Alex's mouth fell open. Inchy hit a duff note. House and Cherry gasped. Tabbris inviting them to do something nice? It was unheard of.

'I'm really very impressed indeed by all this,' continued the old angel. 'It shows tremendous thoughtfulness and care. Angelic qualities indeed. Well done. Perhaps Gabriel is right and there is hope for you after all.'

Spit looked at Alex and nodded purposefully. Alex nodded back and trotted out to the kitchen. He returned two minutes later, his hands empty and his face confused.

'They've gone,' he said.

Spit shot a look at Alex, the sweet smile he had put on for the sake of Tabbris vanishing like a smudge of chocolate wiped away by a damp hanky.

'You what?'

'They've gone,' repeated Alex. 'The scones. They're not there. The whole tray has vanished.'

'Impossible,' said Spit. 'A tray of scones does not just vanish.'

'Well, this one has,' insisted Alex. 'In fact, you could say it's *scone* missing!'

No one laughed.

'Is there a problem?' asked Tabbris, placing down his empty cup.

'No,' said Alex. 'I mean, well, yes, actually there is. The scones have disappeared.'

Narrowing his eyes suspiciously, Spit turned to look at House. As did everyone else.

'It wasn't me!' protested House.

Tabbris raised an eyebrow.

'Seriously!' said House. 'I was only in the kitchen once, and that was when Alex was there, wasn't it, Alex?'

Alex nodded.

Tabbris leaned back in his chair and looked at Alex meaningfully.

'So you were the last person alone with the scones? Where are they, Alex?'

'I don't know,' said Alex. 'I put the extras on the table for later before I came in here. Now they're not there. I don't know what's happened to them.'

Tabbris sighed and stood up.

'How disappointing.'

'I'm telling the truth,' said Alex desperately. 'I didn't eat the scones.'

'And yet they are not there,' said Tabbris. He moved to the living-room door and looked back at the gang, his face thoughtful. 'Another promising occasion spoiled at the end . . .'

And then he was gone.

Silence swept into the room for a moment as the gang stared at Alex accusingly.

'You just couldn't resist it, could you?' said Spit finally, his eyes full of anger. 'You just had to mess things up.'

'I didn't do it,' said Alex, unable to hide the frustration in his voice. 'I didn't.'

'Couldn't you deal with the fact that my idea was actually working, is that it? Where are the scones, Alex? Where are they?'

'Come and see for yourself,' snapped Alex, his temper rising.

Led by Alex, the gang marched into the kitchen. 'See? I left the tray on the table. Now it's gone.'

'And I bet your belly's full,' said Spit.

'Is it wrong for an angel to want to punch another angel?' asked Alex, squaring up to Spit. 'Because at this precise moment, I really don't care!'

Inchy squirmed in between Alex and Spit. 'There has to be a rational explanation for this,' he squeaked.

'There is,' retorted Spit. 'Alex gobbled the lot.'

With a roar, Alex tried to leap for Spit, but House pulled him back. At the same time, Cherry grabbed hold of Spit, tugging him back too.

'For the last time, I didn't eat them!'

Spit stared hard at Alex. 'You just can't cope with not being in charge, can you? When *you* were captain, you were always going on about how I had to be one of the team and support your plans, but now *I'm* leader you just want to spoil my ideas.'

Alex was too angry to say anything. He couldn't believe he was getting the blame.

'Well, you know what,' said Spit, 'I don't care. I don't care that you don't like me being gang leader. And I don't care that you've tried to ruin the first thing we've done since being here that actually impressed Tabbris. But I *do* care about getting us back to Heaven. Can't you see that? And I'm going to do it, with or without your help.'

With that, Spit shrugged Cherry's hand off his shoulder, turned on his heel and walked out.

Cherry shook her head sadly at Alex and then followed Spit out of the room. Everyone else went too.

Everyone except Alex.

Alone in the empty kitchen, he slumped down on to a stool. In front of him, the table stared back, empty apart from a few crumbs. *Someone* had stolen the scones. And he was the only person in the house who knew for a fact it hadn't been him.

Alex stayed in the kitchen until the others had gone to bed. Then he tiptoed up the stairs and lay on his bed in the dark, racking his brains for any idea about what might have happened. When he eventually fell asleep, his dreams were filled with images of scones sprouting little feet and running away, as he chased them with an enormous bent silver knife. It wasn't a fun dream and he never caught the scones.

Pants.

4
Sweet Tooth

'Is it just me, or is this all totally pointless?' asked Alex.

He and Cherry were sitting at the bottom of the stairs, polishing their shoes in preparation for their weekly school uniform inspection.

'How do you mean?' said Cherry.

'Well, apart from Tabbris, who cares if our shoes are perfectly shiny?' Alex wondered. 'And I can just about see why we have to iron our shirts and trousers, but is it really necessary to iron our pants and socks too?'

Cherry said nothing and got back to buffing her shoes. Not that she was going to wear them to school. No way. She didn't want to look a dork. She'd be changing into the boots she had in her bag as soon as the gang were out of sight of Eccles Road.

House arrived, carrying his own shoes.

'Hey, Alex, Cherry . . .'

Alex and Cherry nodded.

'I totally forgot I had to polish these,' said House. 'Budge up.'

Alex and Cherry moved apart and House slipped in between them, grabbed the polish and a rag, and knuckled down.

'I was just asking Cherry,' said Alex. 'Do you think all this cleaning is totally pointless . . .'

Alex's voice tailed away as Spit and Inchy appeared.

'Tabbris doesn't think it's pointless,' said Spit. 'So neither do I. If we start doing what he wants, we'll be back in Heaven much sooner than if we fight against him.'

No one said anything.

Alex was still smarting from the way that none of the others had seemed to believe him about the scones. He'd decided to keep his mouth shut and not get into any more arguments with Spit, no matter how difficult that actually was.

Spit looked down his nose at House. 'You busy?'

'Not really. I've nearly finished my shoes.'

'Excellent,' beamed Spit. 'It's just that I've had so many other things to do, that I haven't been able to do mine, and they really are in a bit of a state. Would you mind?'

Spit dropped his shoes on the floor in front of House. They were caked in mud, with a big scuff down one side.

Cherry looked up at Spit suspiciously. 'What other things have you had to do?'

'Gang leader stuff,' said Spit. 'Improving my working relationship with our angelic guardian, for example. See you at inspection.'

Before anyone could say anything else, Spit had turned and gone, leaving them to their polishing. Cherry looked over at Alex, confused.

'No, I'm not sure what it meant either,' said Alex. 'But I think it might be "Sucking up to Tabbris".'

'Hah,' harrumphed Cherry. 'Well rather him than me.'

'Are you seriously going to do his shoes?' Alex asked House.

House shrugged. 'I guess,' he said. 'If he has been busy . . .'

'But I never got you to do jobs for me when I was captain!' said Alex. 'Why are you letting Spit do it?'

House couldn't think of an answer.

Cherry focused on her shoes.

Inchy stared at something very interesting on the ceiling.

Alex ground his teeth quietly, but if the rest of the gang weren't willing to complain about Spit taking advantage, there was nothing he could say. They were obviously willing to do anything if it meant improving their chances of getting back to Heaven. Lowering his head, Alex buffed at his own shoes furiously for five minutes without stopping, until finally Spit returned with Tabbris in tow.

41

'All right, all right,' rumbled Tabbris. 'Atten-*shun*!'

The gang jumped to their feet and stood up straight and still while Tabbris, his chest puffed out and a very serious look on his face, limped down the line, inspecting them. He scrutinized the creases in their trousers, the shininess of their shoes, and the straightness of their ties. He even checked to see that the insides of their ears were clean.

'Hmmm . . .' he said.

The gang held their breath. They all knew that if one of them didn't meet Tabbris's high standards, they would all be on potato-peeling duty again that night.

'Hmmm . . .' Tabbris said again.

No one moved, not even to blink.

Tabbris stepped back and looked at the gang.

'Well done.'

'What?' said Cherry.

'Not "what"!' barked Tabbris. 'The correct word is *pardon*. And I said "Well done".'

'Are you serious?' asked Alex.

'Oh, I'm always serious,' said Tabbris.

No one disagreed with that.

'You have all done well,' Tabbris continued, now pacing up and down in front of the gang. 'In fact, I think that this is the best turnout you've ever managed. I am both surprised and encouraged.'

For a few stunned seconds, no one said a word. Then Spit spoke.

'Thank you, sir,' he said. 'All we want to do is to show you we really can be good when we try.'

'Of course you can,' said Tabbris. 'And I'm particularly impressed with you, young Respite. Not only do you seem to be leading from the front with your improved attitude, but your shoes are the shiniest I've seen in years. Well done.'

Out of the corner of his eye, Alex glanced over at Spit. Surely he was going to say something about House?

'Thank you,' said Spit, beaming out a smile bright enough to melt glass.

Obviously not.

'Well, off to school with you, young rapscallions,' chuckled Tabbris, who seemed in an abnormally cheerful mood as he ushered them out of the door. 'See you tonight.'

Spit led the way, head held high, as if he was leading a parade. The rest of the gang followed eagerly. Alex trudged along behind muttering darkly to himself. Spit's brown-nosing was getting worse by the day, but he couldn't shake off a horrible growing suspicion.

It might just be working . . .

'No way. I'm not going into the same room as those . . . *things*.'

The gang were standing outside their science classroom trying to reason with Inchy, who was standing with his back to the door, his hands stuffed deep into his pockets.

'Inchy, you have to,' said Cherry. 'They're just rats, that's all. They can't hurt you.'

'Rubbish!' snorted Inchy. 'They can bite you and scratch you and give you the plague.'

'They can't!' laughed House. 'That's you just being silly.'

'Haven't you read about the Black Death?' replied

44

Inchy. 'Festering boils, people dropping dead in the street, mass graves, that sort of thing? All down to rats!'

House's face went pale. 'Are you serious?'

'Deadly serious.'

'But what Inchy isn't telling you,' put in Alex, 'is that this all happened about six hundred years ago.'

'Phew!' House wiped his brow. 'I was getting a bit worried for a minute.'

Spit fixed Inchy with a steely gaze. 'Look, if you don't come in, you'll be in big trouble,' he said. 'And that means we're all in trouble with Tabbris. So get a grip and get inside.'

With that, he strode into the classroom, followed by the others.

Cherry looked back. Inchy hadn't moved, well, an inch. Then she had an idea. Inchy could be very stubborn. It was no good trying to force him to do something he didn't want to. But he did have one weakness . . . Slowly, Cherry walked back to his side.

'What?' demanded Inchy. 'I've said I'm not going in, and that's final.'

'OK,' said Cherry. 'I just thought that . . . No, it doesn't matter.'

'What?' said Inchy, his curiosity getting the better of him.

'I'm just worried, that's all,' sighed Cherry. 'I mean, you know how Spit's taken over from Alex as leader?'

Inchy nodded.

'Well, what if he takes over from you as the brains of the gang too? He's pretty clever, you know. Almost as clever as you. If you keep missing lessons, maybe he'll overtake you.'

Inchy looked at Cherry. 'You really think I'm the brains of the gang? Seriously?'

'Of course,' Cherry put on her best I-think-you're-wonderful smile. 'But maybe not for long, if you don't keep working at it.'

'Right!' Inchy set his jaw determinedly. 'Let's do some learning!'

And with that, he marched past Cherry and into the classroom.

Cherry grinned. 'Like taking candy from a baby . . .'

Inside, the lesson was just getting started. Everyone in class had their cages out and were studying their rats. The gang hurried to pick up their own cage.

'So why are all the other rats bigger than ours?' asked House.

'He has a name,' said Alex sharply.

'Oh yeah, sorry,' said House, rolling his eyes. 'Why is everyone else's rat bigger than, erm, Gerald?'

The gang crowded round the cage. It was true. All the other rats in the class seemed to have grown bigger, and had glossy coats and bright eyes. By comparison, Gerald did look a bit thin and sorry for himself.

'Perhaps he's just embarrassed to have such a naff name,' said Spit. 'It's put him off his food.'

'Ha ha,' said Alex. 'There's nothing wrong with his appetite. Look.'

He pointed at the three feeders strapped to the side of the cage. The one labelled *Cheese* had only a few crumbs at the bottom, the *Peanuts* feeder was only a quarter full, while the one marked *Chocolate drops* was completely empty.

'Looks like Gerald has a sweet tooth,' observed Spit.

'Perhaps he's ill,' said Cherry, sounding concerned. 'His fur's all dull and patchy.'

'I don't think he likes being cooped up,' said Alex. 'I'm going to ask Mr Roddan what's wrong.'

'Are you sure you want to do that?' asked House. 'Just look at him.'

Mr Roddan was sitting behind his desk at the front of the class, looking even more twitchy than usual. He kept running his fingers through his greasy, thinning hair, as if his scalp was really itchy. He seemed to be talking to himself.

'On second thoughts, I'll wait until the end of the lesson,' said Alex. 'Maybe Gerald will perk up a bit.'

For the remainder of the lesson, the gang busied themselves in cleaning out Gerald's cage and refilling his water bottle and feeders, while Gerald just sat forlornly on the corner of Alex's desk, whiskers drooping. Even Inchy felt a bit sorry for him.

When the bell rang, the rest of the gang hastily scooped Gerald back into his cage.

'I'll catch you up,' said Alex. 'I'm really worried about him. I'm going to ask Mr Roddan.'

'Good luck,' said Spit, shaking his head, and the rest of the gang slipped out of the door.

Alex slowly walked up to the front of the class. Mr Roddan was bent over his desk, practically gnawing on an apple. The sound of munching and crunching seemed suddenly very loud in the empty classroom.

'Blimey,' breathed Alex. 'He looks more like a rat than Gerald does!'

Alex reached the desk, but it took a few moments for Mr Roddan to notice he was there. Then suddenly he lifted his eyes and stared warily at Alex. Little dribbles of apple juice slid down his chin, like his mouth was melting.

'Yes?'

'It's about Gerald,' said Alex.

'Who's Gerald?' said Mr Roddan, taking another nibble of apple.

'Our rat,' replied Alex.

'How do you know his name's Gerald?' asked Mr Roddan suspiciously.

'Because that's what we called him.'

'Oh, you did, did you!' Mr Roddan's eyes flashed. 'And what if I gave you a new name, eh? What if I decided that Alex didn't suit you at all, and that you would be much better as a Wayne or a Callum. What then?'

Alex didn't know quite what to say.

'Erm, but he's a rat,' he replied eventually. 'He didn't have a name already.'

'How little you know,' said Mr Roddan with a sneer. He dropped the apple on to his desk and wiped his face with quick little movements that Alex found strangely unsettling. 'What do you want, boy?'

Alex took a deep breath. 'Gerald isn't growing. He looks ill. But all the other rats are fine. Do you know what might be wrong with him?'

Mr Roddan darted down the classroom and peered into Gerald's cage. At the sight of the teacher, Gerald cowered into a corner. He looked, thought Alex, rather like Inchy would have done if confronted with a giant rat five times his own size.

Mr Roddan stared into the cage for a long

moment. Then he wiped his face again, scratched his ears and shuffled his feet.

'Do you think he could have caught a cold or something?' prompted Alex. 'Can rats catch colds?'

'No,' replied Mr Roddan. 'Has he been eating his chocolate?'

'Erm, yes,' replied Alex, rather surprised by the question. 'He cleared out the whole feeder.'

Mr Roddan twitched again. 'Then there's nothing to worry about. He's probably just taking a bit of time to get used to the classroom, that's all. Goodbye.'

And with that, he turned and scuttled out of the classroom door.

The room was quiet except for the scratching, nibbling and sniffing of a dozen rats. Alex looked down at Gerald. The little rat stared back at Alex through dull, tired eyes.

'I don't care what Weirdo Roddan says,' muttered Alex. 'There's something wrong with you. And if the others don't want to help, I'll sort it out myself . . .'

5
Five a Day

Alex walked out of the science block and looked at his watch. The bizarre conversation he'd had with the very strange and rather creepy Mr Roddan had taken longer than he'd thought. Now he'd have to rush across school to avoid being late, and Alex wasn't a big fan of rushing to lessons. At least not here on Earth. It had been different at Cloud Nine Academy, racing House from class to class on their snow-white wings.

Alex closed his eyes, and for a moment he was

suddenly swept back to the days before they'd been sent down to Earth. His shoulders flexed, almost as though phantom wings were attached. And then, in his mind, he was flying. He could feel the wind rushing past, his stomach flipping as he took a steep dive.

Alex opened his eyes and let out a sigh. He didn't like what Spit was doing, but maybe it *was* for the best. The gang had to get back to Heaven as soon as possible. Maybe he could toe the line, and go along with Spit's plan, just for a little while. Even if following Spit's lead was like eating pins for breakfast.

But first, he had to get to class. Alex weighed up his options. If he went the proper way through the main building, he'd definitely be late. But it was either that or take a short cut through the staff car park. But that was strictly off limits. Out of bounds. Naughty. If Spit had been there, he never would have allowed it.

Alex grinned. That settled it, then.

He sprinted through the car park gate and weaved silently through the parked cars, thinking how much easier this would be if he still had his wings and could go *over* rather than round them. In fact, he was so busy thinking about it that, as he turned a corner, Alex had to pull himself to a sharp stop before he ran slap-bang into a delivery van parked at the back of the canteen.

The van was large, ugly and dirty. In fact, it was *so* dirty, Alex had no idea what colour it was actually supposed to be. Its back door was open, as was the door to the canteen. Vast plumes of steam billowed out, bringing odours of chips, boiled cabbage and something that smelled alarmingly like poo.

Alex paused. The canteen food at Green Hill School wasn't exactly brilliant, but it had never smelled *that* bad. He looked around, expecting to see a blocked drain or an open manhole cover, but there was nothing in sight. Alex decided that perhaps he wouldn't be having school dinners today. Or indeed ever again.

Just as he was about to slip away, Alex had to duck for cover as two men emerged from the canteen door. One was short and fat, wearing a cook's jacket and hairnet, the other tall and thin, dressed in overalls and clutching a clipboard.

'It's a bloomin' mystery and no mistake,' said the short man, obviously one of the school chefs. 'You're sure you left 'em by the door as usual?'

'Five bags of prime carrots, as ordered,' replied the tall man. 'I've been making this delivery for six months and I left 'em just where I always leave 'em.'

Alex listened harder, leaning in to catch every word.

'Well, they wasn't here this morning,' growled the chef.

'I hope you're not suggesting I nicked 'em,' said the delivery man. 'I mean, what would I want with five bags of carrots? I ain't a rabbit farmer.'

'Well, I dunno,' sighed the chef, scratching his head. 'I guess I'll have to do sprouts today instead. See ya next week.'

Alex stayed perfectly still as the van pulled away and the chef disappeared back into the canteen, but his mind was whirling. Who would want to steal five bags of carrots indeed? It was a good question, but Alex reckoned that the answer might be *the same person who'd want to steal a large tray of leftover scones . . .*

'That's it,' said House, closing his exercise book and standing up. 'I'm done. And I'm starving. Anyone fancy joining me for a snack?'

The gang were in the study at Eccles Road, finishing off their homework.

'By "joining you", do you actually mean, *have* a snack?' asked Cherry. 'Or watch you eat one?'

House grinned. 'I've got a secret stash of crisps that Tabbris doesn't know about. They're in the bedroom. We can all share them if you like.'

'Sounds good,' said Cherry. 'You lot coming?'

Alex and Inchy got to their feet at once, but Spit just cleared his throat loudly. Inchy turned red and sat down again.

'What's up?' asked Alex.

'Oh, it's OK,' said Inchy, an almost-smile on his face. 'I'm, um, not quite finished yet. I'll grab something later.'

'But you always finish your homework first,' said Alex, walking over. 'What have you got to do?'

'It's nothing . . .' said Inchy. 'Really, it isn't.'

Alex looked at the exercise book on the desk in front of Inchy. He instantly recognized Spit's handwriting.

'What's going on?'

Inchy opened his mouth to speak, but Spit got in first.

'He's doing me a favour, that's all, aren't you, Inchy?'

'He's doing your homework, isn't he?' said Alex, unable to believe what his eyes were telling him. 'Why? It's your homework, Spit.'

'I've been busy,' said Spit with a shrug.

'Busy?' said Alex. 'Doing what? Exercising your ego?'

Spit spread out a large and elaborate diagram across the desk. 'I have been planning tactics for our next football match. It's tomorrow, so pretty urgent, really. And it's taken up a few late nights, I can tell you.'

Alex spluttered a laugh. 'You? But you haven't got a clue! Cherry's the one who does all the tactics, not you!'

'Well, it's me now,' said Spit. 'And I've spent so

much time on it that I just don't have any spare minutes to squeeze in my homework.'

'Rubbish,' said Alex.

'And if, like Inchy, you want us to win, you'll just let him get on, OK?'

Alex would have replied, but Spit had already pushed past him to join the others heading for the bedroom and House's crisps.

He looked at Inchy.

'You should have said no.'

'It's OK,' shrugged Inchy with a weak smile. 'Really it is.'

'It's really not,' Alex replied. 'If you –'

'NOOOOOOO!'

The roar echoed through the house like an explosion.

Alex and Inchy raced out of the study and up to the bedroom. House was on his hands and knees, a look of horror on his face.

'Gone!' moaned House. 'All gone . . .'

'What's going on?' asked Alex. 'What's gone?'

'As if you didn't know, Mr Sticky Fingers,' growled Spit.

'Someone's raided my stash,' whimpered House. 'They've swiped the lot.'

'What?'

'House's crisps,' snapped Cherry. 'They've gone. Someone's taken them.'

'I knew it!' cried Alex triumphantly. 'There's someone in Green Hill stealing food. Carrots were taken from the school canteen and –' He stopped and sniffed the air. 'That smell! The one like drains! It's here as well . . .'

Alex trailed off as he realized that the rest of the gang were staring at him disbelievingly.

'Carrots?' said Spit.

'I'm not making it up,' said Alex. 'I heard the delivery guy talking about it. Bags of carrots have gone missing. Five bags, actually.'

'They may well have done,' replied Spit. 'But I think we all know where they went.'

'You think it's me?' said Alex, stepping back. 'Are you serious? What, twenty scones and fifty kilograms of carrots wasn't enough, so I came back home for some crisps just to finish off?'

'You tell us,' said Spit.

'I *am* telling you!' said Alex. 'It wasn't me!'

'Who was it, then?' asked Cherry.

'Look,' said Alex, trying to keep calm. 'I didn't eat the scones and I certainly didn't eat your crisps, House.'

House didn't look convinced.

'But you're the only one who knew where I kept the crisps,' he observed sadly.

'And you *were* in an awful hurry to get home from school today,' remarked Cherry.

'And you *did* rush straight up to the bedroom when we got in,' added Inchy.

'The evidence all points one way, Alex,' finished Spit. 'To you. What were you up to in the bedroom while we were all still taking our coats off?'

Alex flushed guiltily. But he wasn't going to say anything – this secret was all his to be in charge of. Spit could mind his own business.

'Nothing,' he said lamely.

'Really?' said Spit. 'It doesn't look that way, does it?'

Alex couldn't believe what he was hearing.

Everyone was blaming him for something he hadn't done – *again*.

'You really don't believe me?' he said, facing his friends.

Silence.

'Fine,' said Alex. 'Be like that. Believe that I stole the scones and the crisps – and the carrots too, if it makes you feel better.' He stormed over to the door. 'But it shouldn't make you feel better. Because I didn't do it. And if none of you did it either, then that means somebody else did, doesn't it? And who knows what they'll steal next!'

Slamming the door, Alex stamped down the stairs, across the garden and into the shed. It was freezing cold, but he didn't care. Sitting there in the dark, he remembered how that morning he'd dreamed of being back in Heaven, flying again, swooping and spinning. And how he'd thought about being a good team player and supporting Spit.

But now it seemed that being one of the team didn't help when the rest of that team thought that he was a thief. None of them would take his word that he wasn't.

And there was nothing he could do about it.

6
The Smell of Success

'Remember, team,' said Spit. 'P.M.A.'

The gang were sitting round the large table in the kitchen having breakfast. It was boiled eggs and toast soldiers for everyone. House was already on to his third battalion.

'What does that stand for?' he asked.

'Pretty Mental Angel,' muttered Alex, staring at his breakfast with little interest. He was sitting at the end of the table, as far away from the others as possible.

Spit looked at Alex, his eyes narrowed. 'Very funny. As Alex knows well, it actually stands for *Positive Mental Attitude*. And to win our first match of the season today, all we need is P.M.A.'

'Wings would be rather more useful, don't you think?' said Alex sarcastically.

'I really miss flying,' said House, reaching for his fourth egg.

Inchy looked over at him. 'If you eat any more of those, you won't need wings – you'll fly on gas power alone!'

Everyone laughed.

'Spit's right,' said Cherry, standing up, her breakfast finished. 'Even Tabbris might be impressed if we win. I know he's not interested in footie, but it'll show him how well we can work together.'

Alex looked up. 'What's happened to you, Cherry?'

Cherry looked back at him and crossed her arms. 'Nothing has happened to me, Alex,' she said. 'I just want to get back to Heaven, that's all. And the sooner the better.'

'Are you saying I don't?' said Alex. 'I miss it as much as the rest of you!'

'But what have you done to help us get back there?' asked Spit. He didn't give Alex a chance to answer, but just stood up and walked out.

'Come on, Inch,' said Cherry. 'We'd better get a move on. Don't want to be late.'

Inchy got up and followed Cherry out of the kitchen.

Alex looked across at House. 'Why don't any of you believe me about the scones and the crisps?'

'I never said I didn't,' protested House.

'You never said you did, either.'

House looked up. 'Sorry, mate,' he said. 'It's just . . .'

'Just what?' said Alex.

'Like Cherry said,' explained House, 'I want to get back to Heaven, that's all. And like it or not, Spit's ideas seem to be impressing Tabbris.'

'I guess,' admitted Alex.

House stood up. 'You coming?'

Alex looked at his uneaten egg, then back to House. 'Not hungry anyway.'

* * *

'All right, let's get this over with,' said Inchy, gritting his teeth.

The science lab was quietly abuzz with children collecting their rats. The gang took their seats as Spit went to pick up Gerald's cage from the bench at the front of the class. As Alex watched, one of the boys on the next table pulled off the cover on their cage.

'Whoa!' Inchy jumped to his feet as the rat inside leapt at the bars, gnashing a set of very large, very yellow and very pointed teeth.

'It's enormous!' breathed House.

He was right. The black-and-white rat was at least twice as big as it had been at the last lesson.

'How did their rat get so huge?' said Cherry.

Alex stared around the room. All the other rats were just as big – and just as aggressive. One of them was actually chewing the metal bars of the cage.

'You OK, Inch?'

Inchy just nodded. He seemed to be concentrating on remembering how to breathe.

Spit returned to the table. 'Well, it doesn't feel

like Gerald's grown at all,' he said. 'This cage is as light as a feather.'

He pulled off the cover. The gang gasped.

The bottom of Gerald's cage was filled with clean sawdust. It had a nice little area of soft, cosy wood-shaving bedding for him to snuggle into and fall asleep. A water bottle hung from a piece of wire. The three feeders containing cheese, peanuts and chocolate drops were full and in place. Everything was as it should be. Except for one thing.

Gerald was gone.

Spit leaned in to examine the cage. 'What on Earth is going on?' he said.

Alex grinned. 'He's escaped, by the look of it. Can't say I blame him, really. I told you he didn't like being locked up. Well done, Gerald!'

'I wouldn't be so pleased if I were you,' said Cherry. 'I don't know how well he'll cope out on his own.'

'I bet he's fine,' said Alex confidently. 'He's probably in a dustbin somewhere, scoffing mouldy pizza as we speak.'

A pitter-patter of footsteps announced the arrival of Mr Roddan at the gang's table.

'Is there some sort of problem?' he said in a scratchy voice.

'It's Gerald, our rat,' said Alex. 'He's escaped.'

'Escaped?' snapped Mr Roddan.

At the sound of the teacher's angrily raised voice, the other rats reacted at once, jumping around their cages, snarling and twitching.

Mr Roddan looked around the classroom, his eyes darting from rat to rat. As he stared at them, the rodents slowly settled down.

'How could he escape from a locked cage?' hissed Mr Roddan through his thin, bloodless lips.

'I guess one of us must have forgotten to lock the door,' replied Alex with a shrug. 'Sorry.'

For a moment, Mr Roddan looked like he might leap across the table at Alex. Then he seemed to pull himself together.

'It's just one,' he muttered to himself. 'Just one. Plenty more. Plenty more.' He turned his attention back to the gang. 'Well, since you don't have a rat to look after, turn to page three hundred and twenty-four of your textbooks and work through all the questions in that chapter.'

With that, he turned away from the gang and walked back to the front of the classroom, muttering under his breath again.

'That was weird,' said Inchy.

'How do you mean?' asked House.

'Did you see how the rats reacted to Mr Roddan?' whispered Inchy. 'When he raised his voice they all went mad, then when he stared them out they all went quiet again.'

'It's nothing and it's not important,' said Spit. 'Gerald was just a rat, and Mr Roddan is clearly just a very sad and rather bonkers man. What we need to concentrate on now is the football match!'

'But what about Gerald?' said Cherry.

'I agree with Alex,' said Spit, much to Alex's surprise. 'Gerald will be fine and is better off wherever he is.'

'But –' said Cherry.

'P.M.A. Remember?' said Spit. 'Now let's get on with these questions. The sooner this lesson is over, the sooner we can get out on the hallowed turf of Green Hill School football field. I've got a couple of changes I want to make to our line-up for this match . . .'

'You want me in goal?' said Alex incredulously.

'And me up front?' said House, his jaw dropping.

Spit nodded.

'You're ill in the head,' said Alex. 'House is *way* better than me in goal.'

'And Alex is our striker,' said House. 'It won't work.'

Cherry and Inchy were listening in as Spit explained his plan to the team.

'Look,' he sighed. 'The other team has faced us before. They'll be expecting us to play the same way as we did last time, in the same positions. This will totally surprise them. They'll make mistakes. It's genius!'

'It's suicide,' replied Alex. 'You're a muppet.'

'Trust me,' said Spit. 'I know what I'm doing.'

Alex opened his mouth to say something, but thought better of it.

'That's that, then,' said Spit. 'Come on!'

With that, he jogged out of the changing room

and on to the pitch. Looking about as comfortable as an ostrich on a bicycle, House stepped up to take the kick-off.

He looked back at Alex, who looked equally out of place standing in the goalmouth. He shrugged. Either Spit was right and this was a plan of utter brilliance, or it was a total disaster waiting to happen. There was only one way to find out.

The whistle blew.

With a quick flick, House sent the ball wide to Cherry. One of the opposition was on her, fast as lightning, but what they didn't see was House edge forward, always keeping an eye out to make sure he wasn't offside.

With two players charging down on her, Cherry looked like she was about to be squished.

'Here!' Inchy called. 'I'm unmarked!'

Cherry chipped the ball high over the heads of the opposition, landing it perfectly at Inchy's feet. Inchy checked left, then right, then slotted a precision cross to House.

House swung his foot with such force that Inchy thought the ball would burst.

But it didn't. It rocketed through the air like a guided missile and slammed into the back of the net.

Everyone was stunned.

Spit, Inchy and Cherry raced up to House, throwing their arms round their big friend.

'That was *unbelievable*!' whooped Inchy. 'I've never seen a shot like it! Where did you learn to do that?'

'I don't know,' said House.

'See?' crowed Spit. 'My plan's working. We're going to win!'

'Don't be so confident,' said Cherry. 'The match has only just begun.'

'P.M.A. – remember?' reminded Spit, tapping Cherry on the forehead.

'Do that again and I'll bite your finger off,' warned Cherry, but Spit was already gone, clapping his hands, and didn't hear a word.

'Come on,' grinned Inchy, 'they're ready to kick off again.'

Moments later, the match was back on. And before anyone could do anything about it, House had scored again, this time from a blazing solo run from the halfway line.

'That was awesome!' declared Cherry as House ran back from his second goal, shirt pulled over his head.

'I've never played striker before,' said House. 'I quite like it!'

'What's your secret?' asked Cherry.

'I just hit the ball really, really hard and hope it goes in the right direction,' said House.

Cherry laughed.

House looked back at Alex. He was now sitting on the ground, chewing a piece of grass. Which was why when the other team at last got past House and the rest of the gang, he wasn't ready.

Alex looked up and saw the ball coming. He scrambled to his feet, leapt . . . but it was too late – the ball flew into the goal, to whoops of glee from the opposition.

Spit jogged over. 'Wake up, Alex,' he said. 'What's the point of the rest of us all working hard if you're not even going to pull your weight?'

Alex started to apologize, but Spit had already

turned and gone. He cracked his knuckles with frustration. This was going to be a long match.

'Six-two! Six-two!' warbled Inchy, as the gang walked home after the match. 'What a game!'

'How does it feel to score your first hat-trick, House?' laughed Spit.

'How does it feel, all of you, to have got our best result since we arrived on Earth?' chortled Cherry. 'We *annihilated* them!'

'I told you my plan would work,' said Spit, looking at Alex. 'It was inspired.'

'Lucky, more like,' said Alex sourly.

'That's not very fair,' said Cherry. 'House played brilliantly. We all did.'

'I'm not surprised Alex feels a bit low,' said Spit. 'He did let those two goals in, after all.'

'We still won, though,' said Inchy. 'Thanks to House!'

House flushed with pleasure.

Alex sighed quietly. He did feel pleased for House, but Spit's smugness was just too much to bear. Just as he was wondering if he had ever been quite so smug himself when he was captain, though, something else caught his attention.

'Can you smell that?' he asked, sniffing the air.

'Yes,' answered Spit. 'It's the sweet smell of success.'

'I don't think so,' said Alex. 'It's drains. It's like what I smelled at the school canteen – and in the bedroom after House's crisps went walkabout.'

'Now you come to mention it, it *is* a bit pongy,' admitted Inchy. 'But if there were any nasty niffs around in the bedroom, it was probably House's digestive system that was to blame.'

Cherry guffawed.

'But doesn't it seem weird to you that the smell keeps popping up all over town?' said Alex.

'Not really,' said Spit. 'Drains smell. It's what they do. Particularly if it's been a hot day.'

'But it *hasn't* been hot,' argued Alex. 'And it's not just a normal drain smell, either.'

'I wouldn't know,' said Spit. 'I don't go around smelling drains.'

Alex ignored him, inhaling deeply. 'It's a bit animally. Like a wet dog or something.'

'Ew! Enough!' squealed Inchy. 'That's just nasty.'

Finally, the gang reached Eccles Road and pushed through the front door of number 92.

'So,' said Cherry, 'what are we going to do to celebrate our win?'

'Pig out!' replied House instantly. 'How about pizza?'

'Just so long as we don't get one with tuna on,' said Inchy as they wound their way upstairs.

'What is it about you and tuna?' asked Cherry.

'It's just wrong,' said Inchy. 'And doesn't belong on a pizza. Especially one with pineapple on it.'

'Mmmm . . . pineapple,' drooled House.

Cherry pushed open the bedroom door and swung her bag off her shoulder and on to her bed.

'Whose turn is it to wash the kit?' she asked.

Before anyone had a chance to answer, Inchy interrupted.

With an ear-splitting scream.

7

Thief in the Night

'Inchy!' cried Cherry. 'What is it?'

Inchy was standing at the side of his bed, statue-still, a look of horror frozen on to his face.

'You're white as a sheet,' said Spit. 'What is –'

Then he saw what his friend was staring at.

Sitting on Inchy's pillow, calmly washing his whiskers, was a large brown rat.

'It's Gerald!' shouted Cherry gleefully. 'He's all right!'

'That can't be Gerald,' said House. 'This rat looks

healthy and happy. Gerald was all miserable and thin.'

It was true. The rat on Inchy's pillow looked far perkier than the tired-looking rat they had last seen in his cage back at school.

'It's Gerald all right,' said Cherry. 'He's got the white patch over his eye and everything. He looks bigger than before, though. How can that be?'

'He's probably been eating better since he escaped,' said Alex, his voice strained and awkward.

'Speaking of which,' Spit added, 'getting out of his cage is one thing, but what I want to know is how he got back *here*.'

'Er, guys,' quavered Inchy, who was now shaking like a leaf. 'Can we save the questions until after we have *caught the rat*!'

'Um, I think he heard you,' said Cherry.

The gang turned. Gerald was now standing on his hind legs and staring at them. He seemed to be listening.

'So what do we do?' asked House. 'How do we catch him?'

'I've got a plan,' said Spit. 'GET IT!'

With a roar, Spit, Cherry and House all leapt for the bed. With a squeak of what sounded like excitement, Gerald leapt for the floor.

Cherry hit the bed first, then Spit and finally House.

'Get off!' shouted Cherry from the bottom of the pile. 'You're squashing me flat!'

'What about Gerald?' said House as the gang pulled themselves up. 'Where is he?'

There was no sign of the mischievous rodent, but Alex was laughing fit to burst.

'That was your whole plan, Spit? *Get him?*'

Spit glared at Alex and said nothing.

'I can't believe a rat's been on my pillow, on my *bed*!' squealed Inchy hysterically. 'I'm never sleeping there again. Never!'

'Look!' said Cherry. 'Over there, by the window.'

The gang turned. Against the white of the skirting board, Gerald showed up like a brown stain.

'Grab him!' yelled Spit.

Again he charged forward, hotly pursued by Cherry and House.

With a gleeful chitter, Gerald streaked across the

floor and under Alex's bed. Cherry and Spit managed to pull up before they reached the wall.

Not House. He crashed straight into the radiator with a clang that echoed like a gong.

'We need a new plan,' said House, rubbing his head.

Alex was bent double with laughter. So much for Spit's brilliant powers of leadership. The room was in total chaos. 'I think I might be about to wet myself!' he hooted.

'There!' pointed Inchy. 'It went into the wardrobe!'

'Gerald is a "he", not an "it",' corrected Alex, still chuckling.

'And I'd almost swear he was enjoying this,' muttered Cherry.

'Leave this to me,' ordered Spit. 'He's cornered in there now.'

Slowly, carefully, Spit approached the wardrobe.

'Nice rat, nice Gerald,' he crooned. 'Here, ratty-ratty-ratty.'

Bit by bit, Spit disappeared into the wardrobe. There was a long silence. Then: 'Gotcha!'

Slowly, Spit emerged from the wardrobe. His

black hair was thick with dust and he had a mothball in his ear. But in his right hand, he was holding Gerald.

'It's OK, Inchy,' he said. 'I've got him.'

Inchy gave a sigh of relief.

'I've got something else, though,' continued Spit, his face thunderous.

He held out his left hand, closed into a fist. Then he opened it. Nestled into his palm was a large packet of chocolate drops, just like the ones used in the experiments at school. The packet had clearly been gnawed open and the chocolate inside nibbled.

'I can just about believe that Gerald might have escaped from his cage on his own,' growled Spit. 'But to imagine that he then stole a packet of chocolate drops and hitch-hiked his way halfway across town to take up residence in our wardrobe – that's a bit much to swallow. What's going on?'

'I can explain,' sighed Cherry.

The gang turned to Cherry in amazement.

'It was you?' gaped Spit. 'You aren't just covering for Alex?'

'No, it really was me,' Cherry replied. 'When Roddan gave us that experiment to do, I thought it was a waste of good chocolate to just give it to the rats. So I, er, took some of Gerald's.'

'Some?'

'OK, all.'

'You stole it?' said Inchy. 'But what if Tabbris found out? That's just so totally un-angelic!'

'Don't you think I know that?' snapped Cherry. 'I felt really bad afterwards. I was going to take it back. Anyway, it's disgusting. Doesn't taste like chocolate at all.'

'That's because it's special animal chocolate,' said Inchy. 'You get it in pet shops.'

'Oh,' muttered Cherry. 'Great.'

'But I don't understand why you stole Gerald too?' Spit interrupted.

'I didn't!' said Cherry.

'Pull the other one!'

'I promise I didn't steal him,' said Cherry. 'Really, I didn't. I don't know what he's doing here.'

'You wouldn't,' said Alex. 'Because it was me. I took Gerald.'

For a second or two, no one said anything. Then Spit threw up his hands.

'I'm surrounded by criminals!'

'Look,' replied Alex. 'I just felt sorry for him, that's all.'

'He's a *rat*,' said Spit.

'And he was unhappy,' explained Alex.

'That's no excuse to nick him.'

'I think "rescue" is a better word,' said Alex. 'After I stayed to speak to Mr Roddan, I was left in the room alone with the rats. It was easy, really. Gerald wanted to come.'

'Oh, you can speak to rats now, can you?' said Spit sarcastically.

'It was obvious,' sighed Alex, gently taking Gerald from Spit. 'He looked really bad. I couldn't leave him like that. So I sneaked him out of school and brought him back here. That was why I rushed up to the room so quickly the other day – not to nick House's crisps.'

Gerald gazed adoringly up at Alex, then snuggled down into his hands, curled up into a ball, and went to sleep. He was soon snoring.

'That's louder than House!' said Inchy.

Everyone laughed.

'So what are we going to do with him now?' asked Cherry. 'We can't let him run around free – Inchy will go nuts.'

'He could live in that old bird cage,' said Alex, nodding towards a battered collection of wirework on top of the wardrobe. 'And come out when Inchy isn't around.'

'You sure he won't escape?' asked Inchy.

'Absolutely,' said Alex.

Spit peered at the cage. 'But that still doesn't solve what we're going to do with him, does it? We can't keep a rat here forever.'

'For once, I agree with you,' said Alex. 'Tabbris would go ballistic if he found out. I was only going to keep him until he was healthy enough to be released into the wild.'

'Well, he looks pretty healthy now,' said Spit.

'Just a few more days,' pleaded Alex. 'That's all. Just so we can be sure.'

Spit looked dubious. 'A few days,' he agreed finally.

'Thanks, Spit,' said Alex, gently slipping Gerald into his new home. 'You won't regret it.'

'Ha!' Spit laughed mirthlessly. 'We'll see.'

The sound of a bugle shattered the morning calm.

The gang leapt out of bed as if they had been doused with ice-cold water.

'This is bad,' moaned House as they scrambled into their clothes.

The bugle alarm meant only one thing – Tabbris was angry. Really angry. The last time he had used the bugle to wake the gang up was the morning after Cherry and Inchy had been playing frisbee in the dining room. Using Tabbris's collection of gramophone records as the frisbees.

The sound of their old guardian march-limping up the landing echoed into the bedroom.

'No, no, no,' muttered Spit frantically. 'We've been going so well. What's happened this time?'

The door flew open. Tabbris stared in at them all, his eyes narrow.

'Follow me,' he said. 'At the double.'

Silently, the gang fell into step behind Tabbris.

He led them out of the room, down the stairs and into the kitchen. There, he opened the fridge and removed a plate. He turned to the gang.

'What do you see?' he asked, holding out the plate like a piece of evidence in a trial.

The gang glanced at each other uneasily. No one knew what to say.

'This is not a trick question,' barked Tabbris, his moustache quivering dangerously.

'It's, er, a plate?' said House.

'Well done,' retorted Tabbris sharply. 'A plate. And what is so special about this plate?'

'It's got quite a nice pattern on it?' suggested Cherry.

'It's chipped?' offered Alex.

Tabbris ground his teeth together. It was a sound the gang were more than used to hearing – just before they were about to get a good ear bashing.

'It is an *empty* plate,' said Tabbris. 'See?'

He held the plate out for them all to have a closer look.

'I may be old,' Tabbris continued, 'but I'm not so absent-minded to have placed an empty plate in the refrigerator. In fact, when I put this plate into the refrigerator last night, it had half a cold roast chicken on it. Leftovers from last night's dinner. Yet this morning, it seems that the chicken has vanished.'

'I –' started Alex.

'You will not speak until I say so,' barked Tabbris angrily. 'I'm not interested in excuses. But I am tired of food going missing in this house on what seems to be an increasingly regular basis.

'First the scones, now this,' Tabbris went on, looking at Alex and placing the plate down on the kitchen table. 'Can you at least tell me why?'

'I didn't steal the scones or the chicken!' said Alex. 'Why won't anyone believe me?'

'So you persist in your denial,' Tabbris walked over to Alex. 'Do you have anything further to say?'

'Only that I didn't do it.'

Tabbris shook his head and scrutinized the gang closely. 'I might have known that your recently improved behaviour was too good to be true. Breakfast this morning will be bread and water. As will lunch, dinner and every other meal in this house, until one of you has the decency to own up. That is all.'

Before any of the gang had a chance to reply, Tabbris turned smartly on the heel of his good leg and marched out of the room.

Spit turned to Alex.

'What is wrong with you?'

'With me?' said Alex. 'Nothing! I didn't do it! I was stuffed last night. Why would I steal cold chicken?'

'Well, if you didn't do it, who did?' said Spit. Suddenly, his eyes lit up. 'Gerald!' he hissed.

Without a word spoken, the gang rushed upstairs, charged into their bedroom and over to the wardrobe. Inside the bird cage, Gerald was curled up in a ball, snoring happily. The door of the cage was tightly closed and locked.

'Wasn't Gerald, then,' said Cherry glumly.

'I knew that already,' muttered Alex. 'The scones disappeared before I brought Gerald home, didn't they?'

'What about my crisps?' asked House.

Alex shifted guiltily. 'He was here then, but he couldn't have taken them. Think about it — a rat would've nibbled the packets open and eaten the contents, not stolen the whole thing. And Gerald couldn't have taken the chicken, either — he can't exactly open the fridge, can he?'

'So it *was* you, then,' accused Spit.

'It wasn't me, but I do reckon this is all connected,' said Alex, stroking the snoring Gerald through the bars of the cage. 'The scones, the crisps, the chicken and the disappearing carrots at school.'

'You're mad,' said Spit.

'Well, I didn't steal any of it,' Alex shot back. 'And it seems that the only way to prove to you that I'm telling the truth is to get some hard evidence.'

'And who's going to do that?' demanded Spit.

Alex pursed his lips thoughtfully.

'Me.'

8
Steak Out

Alex waited until everyone was fast asleep before he made his move. It was a night blacker than most, the moon pushed behind thick clouds that carried a threat of rain. Dampness clung to the air.

It had been a long and miserable day. Tabbris had kept his promise about bread and water for breakfast. The gang had hoped to fill up at school, but half the items on the menu weren't available because another delivery of vegetables had disappeared from outside the canteen. While House had practically cried into his mashed parsnips (no potatoes available), it had only made Alex more determined to get to the bottom of the mystery. After a cheerless dinner of, yes, bread and water, the gang had gone to bed early, House's stomach grumbling like an angry volcano.

Opening his eyes, Alex waited for them to adjust to the darkness. Soon he could just about make out the faint shadows of the rest of the room, the deep black shapes of bunk beds and wardrobes and his friends fast asleep. At the other side of the room, a sliver of grey light peeked through the gap under the bedroom door.

Alex sat up slowly. Then swung himself out of his bed, his feet slipping out from under his duvet and into the slippers he'd placed on the floor. He grabbed his dressing gown from the end of the bed and tugged it on. The slippers were soft and the dressing gown thick – Alex knew he would need to be both warm and quiet for what he was about to do.

He breathed slowly and quietly, listening for any signs that his friends had heard him and were awake.

Nothing. Just a faint breathing from Inchy, a gentle snoring from Cherry, a soft sigh from Spit, and a thunderous rumble from House's belly.

Alex slowly edged across the floor, his eyes focused on the bedroom door.

A floorboard creaked.

Alex froze, holding his breath. His heart thumped so loudly he was sure it would wake everyone in the room. But no one stirred, so he continued on his way.

The bedroom door slid open with the faintest of squeaks. Then he was through, the door shut behind him, and he was finally heading down the stairs.

In the silence of the late night, the house felt even bigger to Alex. With every step the walls seemed to grow further away, each step bigger. And all the while his heart kept thumping like a bass drum.

At the bottom of the stairs, Alex edged towards the kitchen. If the only way to prove his innocence was to discover who it was that was *really* responsible for the disappearing food, then that was what he would do. He half wondered if it was

House sleep-eating again. But the big angel hadn't done that since they were back at Cloud Nine, and Alex couldn't believe that the others wouldn't have noticed the crumbs and crusts left on his pillow.

The kitchen door stood ajar. Alex crept in silently and slid into the shadows in the corner of the room. It was cold, but his heavy dressing gown kept out the worst of the draughts, making him cosy enough. Now all he had to do was wait. It wasn't a foolproof plan, he had to admit. There was no guarantee that the real thief would turn up again that night. But he had to try. If necessary, Alex would do this every night until they did. The trouble was, now that he was up, he was hungry.

Bread and water just wasn't enough to keep a young angel going, even if he wasn't as big as Big House. Alex tried his best to ignore his rumbling tummy. He thought about other things, about school, about Heaven, about flying. But everything came back to feeling hungry. Thoughts about school turned into questions about what he was having for lunch. Thoughts about Heaven turned into what he'd eat to celebrate his return. And flying? Well, flying always made him hungry, full stop.

To keep his mind off food, Alex stared into the darkness, willing the thief to turn up and stumble into his trap. That would show the rest of the gang! He tried to imagine how pleased and surprised they would be when he caught the thief red-handed. Tabbris would have to apologize for being grumpy *and* wrong, and he, Alex, would probably be voted back in as gang leader. Brilliant!

Then he yawned. It wasn't a big yawn, or especially loud, but it made him realize just how heavy his eyes felt. After all, it was the middle of the night.

Slowly, Alex's eyes slipped shut.

Gritting his teeth, he opened them again. Forced them wide into a stare. Yes, that was better! It was working! Alex had never felt so awake! He was going to catch the thief, he was sure of it!

His eyes closed again . . .

With a jerk, Alex jolted awake.

He had no idea how long he'd been asleep, and for a few seconds he had no idea where he was.

Then he shivered. His dressing gown was reasonably warm, but it didn't exactly compare to a proper bed.

But it wasn't the cold that had woken him up, Alex was sure of that.

So what was it?

Alex stared into the darkness, listening for anything.

What was that? A scratching sound? Alex leaned forward, straining his ears against the silence of the night.

There it was again! A clear scratch, like nails on metal. And it was coming from the door in the far wall – the back door. Someone was trying to get in!

It was only then that Alex wondered for the first time if his plan was at all sensible. He had no idea who – or what – the thief was. What if they were hardened criminals who thought nothing of using violence to get what they wanted? Here he was, alone, in the dark, in the middle of the night. What if things got out of hand? If he called out, would the rest of the gang be able to reach him in time?

Alex shook his head. This was no time for

negative thoughts. He was an angel! He'd fought demons! He was brave and fearless!

The back door creaked open, and Alex nearly yelled out.

Silhouetted against the night were two small, hunched figures. They weren't much taller than Alex, but there was something strange about the way they moved. As he watched, the pair scuttled into the kitchen. Alex frowned. Humans didn't normally scuttle, even when they were trying not to be seen or heard. They sneaked and tiptoed and skulked, but they didn't *scuttle*.

And neither, Alex realized as he sucked in a nervous breath, did they smell so unspeakably bad.

The reek that followed the two shadows was enough to make Alex choke. It was strong and sour, and horribly familiar – a combination of sewage and wet fur. It crept into Alex's nose and stuck there.

A gust of wind raced past the house and the clouds shifted as rain started to pitter-patter on the window. Then moonlight draped itself over the kitchen and it took all Alex's bravery not to run from the room.

The two figures were human in size, but that was where the similarity ended. They were stooped and hunched over almost double, and they moved in nervous twitches. Their heads were strangely shaped, with pointy snouts, whiskers and fur, and black beady eyes. Fur covered their bodies too, crusted with filth and grime. Every few seconds one of the creatures would scratch at an ear with a clawed hand, or flick the long, pink tail that hung down behind it. And when they spoke, their voices were like the sound of nails being dragged down a blackboard.

'Food,' said the largest rat man, twisting his tail between his furry fingers. 'Get it! Get it!'

The smaller monster skittered over to a cupboard and carefully opened the door.

'Here,' said the large rat man, holding out a grubby sack. 'Fill it. Yes. The food! Fill the sack!'

Nodding silently, the smaller creature started to pull out the contents of the cupboard and stuff them into the sack. Tins of tomatoes followed packets of spaghetti and jars of marmalade. The creature worked fast, but very quietly.

'Someone will notice,' squeaked the small rat man nervously. 'All this food gone? They'll notice. They'll notice!'

'The engine needs it,' said his partner forcefully. 'More food. No time. Get it! Quick! Have to go! Power the engine!'

'Yes, yes, yes, yes. Look – no more left now. Hurry out! Hurry!'

The rat men turned away from the cupboard, closing it behind them, and headed for the door. As they walked across the kitchen, though, their stench once again wafted past Alex. The smell was awful. Before he could stop himself, Alex realized he was going to sneeze. He muffled his face in the arm of his dressing gown, but he knew it wouldn't do any good.

'Aaaa-choooo!'

The rat men stopped.

'Wassat?'

'Wasswot?'

The larger of the two monsters raised his snout into the air and sniffed.

'Someone here,' he growled.

Alex froze. He felt so brittle with terror that he imagined he'd just break into tiny pieces if they even touched him.

The smaller rat man peered through the darkness, his sharp eyes picking out Alex's hiding place in a flash.

'There!' he squeaked. 'There! There!'

The larger rat man bared a set of vicious-looking yellow teeth. Then, before Alex had time to react, he raised a hairy paw and smashed something on the floor. Smoke gushed out and, in a split second, the kitchen was filled with a thick, grey-green fog. When it had cleared, the hideous thieves were gone.

9
Cage Break

'I'd like to say I believe you,' said Spit, looking at Alex. 'But it would be an utter lie.'

The gang were sitting around the breakfast table, while House finished hoovering up the last few crumbs.

'Why would I make it up?' said Alex. 'Rat men? I mean, come on!'

'I agree,' replied Spit. 'It sounds totally ridiculous. Which is exactly what it is, isn't it? Ridiculous.'

Alex felt like he might weep with frustration. After

his encounter with the stinky rat men, he'd crept back to bed and slept badly. In the morning, he'd found it difficult to speak to anyone, the memories of the night still sitting on his shoulder, whispering to him. Then at last, as the gang were finishing breakfast, he'd just blurted it all out – his plan to stake out the kitchen, the arrival of the rat men, the fresh theft, and their final disappearance. And still no one seemed to believe him. He wanted to scream.

'I promise I didn't make it up,' said Alex.

'Perhaps it was a nightmare?' said Cherry. 'Are you sure you didn't just dream it?'

'No, I didn't,' said Alex, through clenched teeth. 'I saw them. They were part rat, part man. And they were stealing food and were talking about an engine or something. Then they disappeared.'

'It wouldn't be the craziest thing that's happened to us since we've been on Earth, would it?' mumbled House through a mouthful of toast. 'I mean, if you compare it to goblins in the woods and zombies in the hospital, rat men in our kitchen doesn't sound quite so weird.'

'I wonder . . .' mused Inchy.

Everyone turned.

'You believe him too?' asked Spit.

'You've heard of the Great Fire of London?' Inchy said.

Everyone nodded.

'Well, at the time of the fire, there were rumours of rat men appearing in London. They were known as Skitterlings — a cross between man and rat. Most people thought that it was mass hysteria brought on by the terrible fire — people seeing things in the smoke.'

'See?' said Spit. 'Hysteria! That's exactly what it is!'

'I'm not so sure,' Inchy replied, shaking his head. 'What if they do exist? Rats are very good at hiding away and not being seen. What if these Skitterlings have just managed to stay out of sight all these years?'

'But that's insane!' said Spit. 'You can't really believe it.'

'I agree with Inchy,' said Cherry. 'It's too mad for Alex to have just dreamed it. Plus all the weirdness with the food disappearing. It does sort of fit.'

'What do you think, House?' asked Alex, turning to the one friend he could always count on.

'All I know is that someone or something is getting to food before me,' said House. 'Rat men or not, I want to find them and have a little word, if you know what I mean?'

Alex grinned.

Inchy looked at Alex. 'This engine thing the Skitterlings mentioned. What exactly did they say about it?'

Alex shrugged. 'Only what I've told you. Something about it needing lots of food to power it. Then I sneezed and they disappeared.'

'Engines don't run on food,' said Spit. 'Everyone knows that.'

'Not true,' retorted Inchy. 'Rotting food gives off a gas called methane. And that gas can be used to power generators, engines, whatever, really.'

Spit went quiet.

'So what are we going to do?' asked Alex. 'If these Skitterling creatures are stealing food to power some kind of engine, then how are we going to find out what it's for?'

Before anyone had a chance to answer, the voice of Tabbris bellowed through the house.

'Oh-eight-fifteen hours! Time for school party to depart!'

'Best get going,' said Cherry.

'We can talk about this on the way to school,' nodded Alex. 'We need a plan.'

'And I'll be thinking of one,' said Spit defensively. 'I am leader, after all.'

'Really?' said Alex, pretending to be surprised. 'I don't think you've mentioned that yet!'

The gang quickly tidied up the kitchen, then dashed into the hall and grabbed their bags.

'Don't be late!' came Tabbris's voice again. 'And stay out of trouble!'

Everyone headed for the front door, but Spit called them to a halt.

'What now?' asked Alex.

'Single file,' said Spit. 'Tabbris likes things all neat and tidy, so we're going to walk to school in single file.'

'I want to say that you can't be serious,' said Cherry, 'but you are, aren't you?'

Spit nodded. 'I'll take the lead,' he barked. 'Hold this, please!'

And before Cherry could say anything, Spit had handed her his bag and walked to the front door. 'Follow me!' he called, and strode off.

Alex looked at Cherry. 'You're not really going to carry that for him, are you?'

Cherry made a face. 'I'd rather stick it somewhere he'd find hard to pull it out of,' she admitted. 'But if I do, Tabbris will just use it as another excuse to have a go at us. So I'll take it for now, but I'm getting a bit tired of fetching and carrying for our illustrious new leader . . .'

With that, she swung the bag up on to her shoulder and marched after Spit.

Inchy, House and Alex quickly followed.

House looked at Alex. 'You're serious about those rat men, aren't you?'

Alex nodded.

'I never really thought it was you who'd stolen stuff,' said House seriously. 'It's not the kind of thing you'd do. Ever.'

'Thanks,' grinned Alex.

'Quick march! Move it! Move it!' screeched Spit from the front of the line.

'You know what,' observed House. 'I think Spit is so desperate to please Tabbris that he's actually turning into him.'

Alex stifled a giggle.

'Now that would be rubbish,' he said. 'A mini-Tabbris? No thanks.'

House laughed. 'He'd inspect the inspections!'

'We'd have to line up before lining up!'

Inchy turned round. 'We'd better hurry up. Spit's way ahead.'

'He's certainly *something* in the head,' said Alex. 'Come on!'

'What happened?' asked Cherry, her jaw hanging open.

The science classroom looked like a bomb had hit it. It was a scene of total chaos. Straw and food was scattered across the floor and under the desks. Posters and notices had been ripped off the walls and shredded. The rat cages looked like a tiger had been at them. The wires were broken and bent out of shape, as if something huge had pulled them apart from the inside. And the rats weren't anywhere to be seen.

'I'm glad I took Gerald when I did,' said Alex, crouching down to take a closer look at one of the ruined cages. 'What on Earth has been going on?'

'Over here!' called Inchy from the other side of the room. 'Look at this!'

The gang walked over. At Inchy's feet was a footprint. It had five toes, the middle three closely bunched together. It was clearly the footprint of a rat. Only it was *enormous*. The size of a cat's paw, perhaps even larger.

'It's impossible,' said Spit.

'True,' agreed Inchy. 'But that doesn't do anything to stop the fact that it exists.'

'The rat that made it must have been humongous!' boggled Cherry.

'But not as large as the rat men I saw at Eccles Road,' said Alex. 'Their footprints would be more like human size.'

As none of their classmates had yet arrived, the gang quickly scouted around the class, looking for any clue as to what could have happened. But all they found was more destruction, and more of the huge rat footprints.

'Where's Roddan?' asked House. 'He's usually here when we arrive, but there's no sign of him.'

'Let's try his office,' said Alex. 'We should tell him what's happened.'

'Hang on,' objected Spit, as Alex headed for the door. 'I'm in charge here. I decide what we do next, right?'

Alex looked at Spit. 'OK, boss,' he said. 'What do you think we should do?'

Spit frowned seriously and stood for a few seconds as if deep in thought. At last, he looked up. 'Ah yes,' he said. 'It's clear to me now. We should go and visit Mr Roddan's office!'

Without waiting for the rest of the gang, Spit turned and left.

'The boy's a genius,' said Alex, following behind.

'Yeah, scary, isn't it?' laughed Cherry.

The gang raced down the corridor to Mr Roddan's office, which was only a few doors away. Spit knocked loudly. There was no answer.

'Mr Roddan,' he called, opening the door a crack. Still nothing.

'OK, follow me,' he said finally, pulling the door wide and walking inside.

Mr Roddan's office was only slightly less chaotic than his classroom. Huge piles of textbooks loomed over the gang like skyscrapers, while stale sandwiches and mouldy cups of coffee lay scattered about on every surface.

'Look!'

House pointed to a rare patch of clean floor. Another of the giant rat footprints stared up at the gang.

'Seems like they came in here,' said Inchy with a shudder. 'Maybe they're still lurking around!'

'Thanks for that thought,' replied Spit grimly. The rest of the gang looked around carefully, but there was no sign of the oversized rodents.

'What's this,' asked Cherry. She had reached Mr Roddan's desk. Sitting on top of it was a large and mysterious-looking brown glass bottle.

The rest of the gang joined Cherry at the desk.

'Looks like the sort of bottle you keep chemicals

109

in,' said Inchy. 'You know, for practical experiments and stuff.'

He reached for the bottle, but before he could slip his fingers around it Cherry let out a strangled gasp.

'Look!' she squeaked. 'There's something under the desk!'

'Is it one of the rats?' asked Alex, ducking down to see.

A pile of tattered brown cloth lay on the floor beneath Mr Roddan's desk.

'Looks like a pile of rags,' he said. 'And smells like rat wee.'

'That's not rags,' said Inchy, looking closer and holding his nose. 'Don't you recognize the material? It's corduroy. It's Mr Roddan's jacket!'

'But it's been torn to shreds,' murmured Cherry. 'Ripped apart! It's as though . . . No, I can't say it.'

'Then I will,' said Alex. 'It looks like Mr Roddan has been eaten by giant rats!'

10
Man Eaters

'What a horrible way to go,' grimaced Cherry. 'I know we didn't really like him much, but he didn't deserve that.'

'How long do you think it took them to eat him?' asked House.

'Depends on the number of rats,' said Inchy. 'And how big they were.'

'Good point,' noted Alex.

'No, it's not!' said Spit. 'And I can't believe we're

even considering the idea that rats ate one of our teachers! That's just impossible!'

'Then you explain the ripped jacket,' said Alex.

'And the empty rat cages,' added House.

'And the giant footprints,' said Cherry.

'But it's insane!' said Spit.

'No more so than demons and zombies and goblins,' said Inchy. 'You've got to admit, they were all pretty insane, yet all completely real.'

Spit couldn't respond to that, so just kept quiet.

'Look here,' said House, picking up a bag from the desktop. 'These were with the bottle.'

'Chocolate drops,' breathed Cherry.

'They look like the ones Gerald was scoffing in the wardrobe back home,' said Alex. 'The ones we were meant to be using in the experiment.'

Inchy looked again at the brown bottle. A horrible idea leapt into his head.

'What if Mr Roddan's been putting something into the chocolate? Something that changes the rats. Makes them bigger.'

Spit laughed. 'So now Mr Roddan's a mad scientist producing Frankenstein rats? That ate him?'

'Do you have a better explanation?'

Spit was silent.

'OK,' he said finally. 'What do we do now?'

Inchy picked up the brown bottle. 'We've got to analyse this. Fast.'

The rest of the school day seemed to crawl by. Each of the gang were secretly racking their brains for a better reason for what they'd found in the science classroom than man-eating rats, but nothing else seemed to make sense.

As soon as the last bell went, the team grabbed their coats and bags and practically ran home. Alex was the first to reach the house, but as he opened the front door he was nearly knocked down by a man coming the other way. He was big and burly and carrying lots of pipes.

'Plumbers,' said Inchy, as three other men followed the first, all carrying more pipes, spanners and other dangerous-looking tools.

'I think they've been fixing the bathroom,'

explained Spit. 'Tabbris has ordered all these new, very posh marble fittings. It's going to be the bathroom of his dreams, apparently.'

'Only Tabbris could get excited about choosing new taps,' grumbled Alex.

'Whatever makes him happy makes me happy,' replied Spit.

'Right,' said Inchy. 'I'm going to get on with checking out the liquid in that bottle we found on Roddan's desk. Tabbris has an old chemistry set in the cellar. It's from before the Second World War, but it still might be useful.'

'Hold on,' called Spit as Inchy turned to go.

'What?'

'I've been thinking,' said Spit. 'Analysing that liquid could be dangerous.'

'So?' said Inchy.

'So,' replied Spit, 'I think I should be the one doing the analysing. Just in case. Leading from the front. Know what I mean?'

'Not really,' interrupted Alex. 'Inchy is the brains in this outfit. He should be the one doing the testing.'

'Look,' said Spit, 'I'm just looking out for everyone's best interests. I should do the testing because that's what proper leaders do, isn't it?'

'"Looking out for our best interests"?' said Alex quietly. 'Don't you mean "Taking all the glory"?'

Spit ignored him. 'Besides, Inchy should be practising his harp, in case we need to charm Tabbris again,' he pointed out. 'So while I test what's in the bottle, he can do that. Meanwhile, you three,' continued Spit, pointing at the others, 'can finish my maths homework. I don't think I'll have the time.'

Snatching the bottle from Inchy's hands, Spit was gone before Alex had the chance to tell him exactly where he could stick his maths homework.

'I don't believe him,' fumed Cherry.

'Yeah, why should he get to do all the fun jobs,' grumbled Inchy. 'I'm supposed to handle the academic stuff.'

'Maths!' moaned House. 'Why did it have to be *maths* homework?'

Alex stared at the others without sympathy.

'Well, you guys agreed to him being leader,' he pointed out.

115

'Yeah,' sniffed Cherry. 'Not one of our greatest moves.'

'Right, harp practice,' Inchy sighed, shuffling over to the corner of the room where his harp stood. He strummed the strings, then played a quick jig.

'Look,' said House. 'Check out Gerald!'

Gerald was still in his cage on the top of Alex's wardrobe, but he seemed to be bouncing up and down in time to the music.

'He's dancing!' grinned Cherry. 'How cute is that?'

Inchy strummed his harp again. Yep, Cherry was right, Gerald was definitely responding to the music.

'Well, at least someone's enjoying my playing,' he said. 'Even if it is only a rat.'

For the next hour or so, the gang carried out their various tasks. Alex, Cherry and House managed to sort out Spit's maths homework, while Inchy played through his entire musical repertoire, much to Gerald's delight. The little rat continued to jive merrily to the faster tunes and, when Inchy played a slower number, he sank into the corner of his cage and listened sleepily, his tail gently beating time against the bars.

It was just before tea when Spit burst through the bedroom door.

'Look!' he yelled, brandishing a bunch of very large flowers. So large in fact, that they practically obscured his whole head.

'I never knew you cared,' growled Cherry. 'I'm touched.'

Spit ignored Cherry and walked into the middle of the room. The rest of the gang gathered round.

'So have you brought the flowers for a reason?' asked Alex. 'Or is it your way of apologizing for just being you?'

Spit sneered at Alex. 'Look closely at them,' he said. 'Notice anything?'

'They're yellow and white and flowery,' said House.

'Anything else?'

'Er . . .'

Spit handed one of the flowers to Inchy. 'Look, you're supposed to be the clever one. What do you see?'

Inchy took the flower, peered at it, then gasped.

'It can't be,' he breathed.

'Can't be what?' said Cherry. 'What is it? What's wrong?'

Inchy looked at the flower, then at Spit, then at the rest of the gang.

'This is a daisy,' said Inchy.

'What, like girls make chains out of?' demanded House incredulously.

'Exactly.'

'But it's the size of a sunflower!' protested Alex. 'It can't be a daisy.'

'It is,' said Spit. 'I put some daisies in a test tube and watered them with a few drops of the liquid from the bottle. This is what happened.'

The gang stared.

'Accelerated growth,' murmured Inchy. 'So, whatever's in that bottle, Mr Roddan must've been adding it to the chocolate.'

'Exactly,' said Spit.

'But that doesn't make sense,' objected Alex. 'All the other rats started growing really quickly, but Gerald only started growing after I stole him.'

'Exactly!' said Inchy.

'Exactly what?' said Alex.

Inchy turned to Cherry. 'When did you start stealing Gerald's chocolate?'

'I can't remember,' said Cherry.

'Come on,' said Spit. 'This could be important.'

'OK,' sighed Cherry. 'From the very first day. I pretended to put the drops in his feeder, but instead I put them in my pocket. Happy now?'

'See?' said Inchy. 'We thought he was eating them because there were none in his feeder at the next lesson, but it was actually Cherry!'

'Imagine if you'd eaten the chocolate, Cherry,' laughed Alex. 'You'd have ended up growing like Inchy back at Halloween!'

Cherry grimaced as she remembered how a magical wish gone wrong that night had started Inchy growing, until he was taller than the trees in Green Hill Woods.

'So what now?' asked Spit.

'Well, first we should stop Gerald eating any more of the chocolate,' said Inchy. 'He's already bigger than he was yesterday.'

House walked over to the cage and removed the last few chocolate drops from Gerald's food dish.

'So why do you think Mr Roddan was doing it, then?' he asked. 'Why would he give the rats something that turned them into bizarre monsters that ate him?'

'Whatever his plan was, I'd guess that wasn't part of it,' said Cherry.

'Right,' agreed Alex. 'And what worries me is what this all has to do with those rat men I saw in the kitchen.'

'The Skitterlings?' said Inchy.

Alex nodded. 'Giant rats are one thing. But rat men? Rat *people*?'

'Big trouble,' said House. 'We're in big, big trouble.'

II
Change of Command

The next day, Spit once again led the increasingly reluctant gang in single file, from Tabbris's house to school. It was a grey morning, the streets filled with a thick fog.

'Can you smell that?' said Alex as they walked through the centre of Green Hill.

'Impossible not to,' remarked Spit, wrinkling his nose. 'What is it?'

'It's the smell of the Skitterlings,' said Alex. 'Drains and wet fur. But worse. It's stronger now.

And it's everywhere – they must have been foraging for food all over town.'

'Whatever it is, it makes me want to puke,' observed Cherry.

'How delightfully put,' said Inchy as the school gates loomed at them out of the fog.

The gang walked through the gates and into the school. The playground was empty.

'That's weird,' said Cherry. 'More people should be here by now.'

'Maybe they're inside,' suggested Inchy as the gang pushed through the main door.

The sight that greeted them inside was not what they were expecting.

'What happened?' said Cherry.

The gang edged forward, pushing through crowds of dazed pupils. The rows of lockers that lined the entrance hall had all been forced open. Lockers were smashed, lying on the floor, or leaning against each other like drunk dominoes. The floor was strewn with books, pencil cases, PE kits and lunchboxes, as if all the cupboards in the school had vomited their contents across the tiles.

It was eerie. The school was strangely quiet, the open locker doors hanging loosely on their hinges, like mouths yawning in collective boredom. Everywhere, teachers and pupils seemed unable to take it all in, searching silently among the crazy mess for anything that they recognized.

House let out a loud groan.

'Oh no! Look!'

Alex looked to where House was pointing.

The tuck shop looked as if it had exploded. Bits of chocolate, burst crisp bags and leaking cans of fizzy pop were scattered everywhere. House stumbled towards it, almost crying.

'It's not that bad, House,' said Alex, running along to catch up with him. 'There are other places to buy food.'

'I know,' sobbed House. 'But it's the waste, you know? All those crisps that will never get eaten. All those cans that'll never get drunk. Why, Alex, why?'

Before Alex could reply, a teacher came bustling up and shooed them all into registration.

'Come along, come along,' she twittered. 'Just

because the tuck shop has been burgled, that doesn't affect lessons!'

'Of course not,' muttered Alex. 'That would be a disaster, wouldn't it?'

Things went from bad to worse at lunchtime. Alex had just about calmed House down enough for the gang to get to their first couple of lessons. But when the bell rang and they headed down to the canteen, the team were brought up short by the sight of the doors firmly closed. A note was pinned up to one of them.

'What's it say?' asked Cherry curiously.

Alex read aloud. '"*CANTEEN CLOSED DUE TO THEFT OF FOOD*".'

'No!' yelled House. 'It can't be! It's not fair! How am I going to survive, Alex? How?'

Spit walked forward, pushing past Alex.

'It's only food,' he said. 'Pull yourself together, House.'

Alex felt House tense up and made sure he had a strong hold of him. 'Don't rise to it, mate,' he said. 'It's just Spit showing his caring leadership style.'

'This isn't the work of thieves,' Cherry said. 'Not normal ones anyway. I know we're all thinking the same thing.'

'Don't say it,' said Inchy.

'Skitterlings,' muttered Alex. 'This is getting out of control.'

'I said not to say it,' said Inchy with a sigh. 'But you're right.'

'OK, well, since lunch is off,' said Alex, ignoring House's moan of protest, 'that gives us a whole hour to investigate what went on here last night. We need to get to the bottom of this and we're better qualified to do it than anyone else.'

'Oh really,' sneered Spit, turning on Alex. 'And that's because you're a trained police officer, is it?'

'This isn't something the human police are going to be able to handle, is it?' replied Alex. 'It's supernatural – angel business. We've saved Green Hill from three supernatural catastrophes. We've dealt with demons and zombies and goblins. I'm thinking we can handle a few overgrown rats!'

'Pah!' said Spit. 'We should leave all of this to

the relevant authorities to sort out or not. Our priority is to get back to Heaven.'

'No, it isn't,' said Alex. 'We're angels. We have a responsibility. We can't leave Green Hill at the mercy of whatever's going on here. It's not what angels do.'

'And what are angels supposed do, Alex?' asked Spit sarcastically.

'We put others before ourselves and protect humans from bad stuff,' said Alex. 'How's that grab you for starters?'

'All right,' sighed Spit. 'I suppose it can't hurt to have a look round during the lunch hour. But don't get carried away. We have to be in art at one thirty.'

'Sure, boss, no problem,' grinned Alex. 'Come on, House. The carrots disappeared from round the back of the canteen; let's check it out.'

It didn't take Alex and House long to find a clue that had them both running back to the others.

'Footprints,' said Alex, trying to catch his breath. 'Not like the ones in Roddan's classroom, though. Proper big ones – Skitterlings. Leading away from the canteen. You won't believe where they go. Come on.'

Inchy, Cherry and a reluctant Spit followed Alex and House round the school to the rear of the canteen. At the back door they saw the footprints.

'Looks like they lead into those bushes at the edge of the footie field,' said Inchy.

'They do,' replied Alex.

The gang edged forward, following the footprints into the bushes and their final destination.

'Oh no.' Cherry's face fell.

The trail of footprints led to a large black hole. Staring down into it the gang could see it was the start of a tunnel. The roots of bushes and trees hung down from the roof like grey, spidery hair, damp and lifeless.

'I don't like it,' said Inchy. 'If the Skitterlings have gone underground, they could be anywhere.'

'I know,' said Alex. 'For all we know they have tunnels all over the place. It's probably how they've been moving about without being seen.'

'But what are they doing?' asked Cherry.

'And why do they need all that lovely food?' said House.

'The only way to find out is to investigate,' Alex

said thoughtfully. 'We'll need torches and boots and stuff like that. And I reckon we should work out a way of keeping an eye on where we are in the tunnel. Perhaps leave a trail of paper or something, or take a length of string and tie it to one of these bushes. Just to help us find our way out again.'

'Right, enough of the Hansel and Gretel nonsense,' snapped Spit.

'Ham and what?' said House, perking up instantly.

'It's time to get back to lessons,' said Spit decisively. 'And then, in case you've all forgotten, we've got our next football match after school tonight.'

Alex groaned. He *had* completely forgotten.

'So, all things considered, this is not the time for us to go charging off on another one of Alex's madcap missions.'

'Madcap?' said Alex.

'Maybe the Skitterlings are down that hole, maybe they're not,' said Spit. 'But we have to finish lessons and play the match before we do anything else. If we don't, Tabbris will hear about it and it will be another black mark.'

'Don't you think finding out what the Skitterlings

are up to is just a little bit more important than art?' asked Alex, doing his best to disguise his annoyance. 'Or even a football match?'

'Match first,' said Spit. 'Then we can talk about what happens next. OK?'

Alex could feel a fountain of objections trying to force its way up his throat and out of his mouth, but, with a titanic effort, he managed to stop it. He just had to face it – Spit was still in charge. It was up to him to decide what to do. It was some small consolation to see that the rest of the gang looked as unhappy with Spit's decision as Alex was, but not much.

'Good,' said Spit. 'So, back to class and then meet me in the changing rooms. We need to discuss our game plan . . .'

'Come on, Cherry, keep moving – no pain, no gain!' bellowed Spit, clapping his hands energetically.

'If he doesn't shut up, I'll show him the true meaning of pain,' snarled Cherry, leaping into mid-air to clear a cross.

The gang were halfway through the match, but

the score remained nil–nil. The teams were evenly matched and there had been a few near misses. Alex was still playing in goal, but itching to get out and back up front. Spit's new formation didn't seem to be working quite so well as last time.

This might have had something to do with the fact that while House, Cherry and Inchy were running their socks off, making probing runs and on-target shots, Spit was doing little more than shouting instructions and motivational slogans. It was as if he had taken the role of manager rather than player. Alex wasn't sure that he'd seen Spit so much as *touch* the ball all game. It felt like they were a man down, and Alex was getting more and more frustrated, not least because he couldn't stop thinking about what the Skitterlings were up to and where their mysterious tunnel might lead.

A shout brought Alex back to the present. He looked up to see Cherry waving and pointing. The ball was flying down the pitch towards his goal. He jumped to intercept, but Spit's voice smashed his concentration.

'Remember, there's no "I" in team!'

Distracted, Alex fumbled the ball. It shot out of his hands, hit the crossbar, just millimetres from slipping into the net, and bounced over the goal and out of play.

'Thanks, Spit,' shouted Alex as the ref called for a corner. 'I could've taken that.'

'Don't make excuses,' said Spit. 'Just play. There's no such thing as a friendly match, right?'

Alex growled, forcing his mind back on to the game. As the corner was taken, he leapt up above a jumping opponent and punched the ball clear. House seized on the opportunity, secured the ball and raced up-field.

It was a brilliant counter-attack. Building up momentum, House pulled away from the chasing defenders. Alex held his breath. It could be the first goal of the game, with only fourteen minutes left to play. House was past the halfway line. He was onside. This was it . . .

Then a thunderous groan rumbled through the ground and House vanished.

Alex did a double-take. What had happened? One second House had been just about to slam the ball home for a seriously cool goal, and the next minute he'd gone!

'House!' yelled Alex, racing towards the spot where he'd last seen his friend.

He was running so fast that he only just managed to skid to a halt as a huge, yawning rupture in the pitch appeared in front of him. A whole section of turf had just sunk into the ground. It was like looking into a giant's footprint.

'Mate!' called Alex. 'House!'

'I'm down here,' replied a voice from inside the hole.

Alex leaned forward and looked down. And at the bottom of the pit, looking unhurt but very confused, sat House.

'You OK?'

'Yep,' said House. 'But I'm not sure how to get out. I've still got the ball, though. If the ref hasn't noticed, I could just chip it up and you could go on to score.'

'I think he's noticed,' said Alex. 'Everyone has.' Then he saw something. 'Hang on,' he said, pointing into the hole. 'What's that over there?'

House jogged over to the place Alex was indicating. 'Looks like part of a tunnel,' he said. 'Shall I go in and have a look?'

'Not on your own and not while everyone else is around,' said Alex. 'Here, give me your hand.'

Scrambling up the side of the pit, House reached out for Alex's hand. With a lot of effort, he managed to haul himself out just as the rest of the team ran up.

'The match is suspended,' said Spit. 'We've got to go back to the changing rooms while the ref sees if there's another pitch available. What happened?'

'Look – there's a tunnel down there.' Alex pointed down the foot-shaped hole. 'It must be the Skitterlings. Their tunnelling has weakened the pitch. Us running around playing football on top of it must have been enough to cause it to collapse.'

The gang turned and walked back to the changing rooms. As Cherry and House pulled off their muddy boots, Alex paced up and down manically.

'We're going to need torches,' he muttered. 'We'll have to go back to Eccles Road.'

'Why?' asked Spit.

'Isn't it obvious?' said Alex. 'If the Skitterlings

have been tunnelling all over town, who knows where the next tunnel might collapse. What if it's under somebody's house? Or a busy road? People might get hurt, even killed. We've got to investigate the tunnels *now*.'

'If we go now and the ref finds another pitch, then we'll forfeit the game.' Spit looked horrified at the very thought.

'So?' snapped Alex. 'It's just football.'

'It is *not* just about football!' said Spit, his voice hard. 'Tabbris wants us to behave well. And if we go after these Skitterlings and get caught, all our good work with the afternoon tea and the uniforms will be undone! We'll be stuck down here forever.'

'Oh, come on,' exploded Cherry. 'We can't just ignore it. Some leader you've been – always taking the soft option. I preferred it when Alex was in charge.'

Alex looked at Cherry, his eyebrows raised in surprise.

'You may have always been getting us into trouble,' she explained, 'but at least it was fun, and at least everyone pulled their weight.'

'What do you mean by that?' asked Spit.

'She means,' said Inchy, 'that Alex didn't just tell us all what to do the whole time.'

'He was one of the team as well as being leader,' added House. 'You just like bossing the rest of us around and getting us to do all the pants things you don't want to do – like maths homework!'

'But I'm just trying to get us back to Heaven!' spluttered Spit. 'Have you forgotten that's what this is all about?'

'To be honest,' said Alex, 'if I can't get back to Heaven by being an angel and doing my job, then I don't want to go back.' He looked at House, Inchy and Cherry. 'So, who's for a bit of tunnel exploration, then?'

'But I'm leader,' shouted Spit, stamping his foot with fury. 'He can't just take over.'

Cherry eyed Spit sourly. 'Wanna bet? All those in favour of having Alex as leader again?'

Inchy, House and Cherry thrust their hands towards the sky.

Alex winked at Spit. 'No hard feelings, eh? Now come on!'

12
Ratnapped!

'Tabbris is fast asleep by the fire,' reported House. 'And snoring.'

The gang were in their bedroom in the old house on Eccles Road. They'd all dashed back from school as fast as they could (well, all except Spit, who'd dragged his feet the whole way) and were now getting their kit together for the tunnel exploration.

Alex grinned. He was back in the role he loved more than anything – leading the gang into adventures. OK, so in the past some of the adventures had turned into nightmares, but that just made life more interesting.

'Good,' he beamed. 'And we all know he sleeps like the dead. So let's get our stuff together and head out.'

'Whatever you say, O mighty leader,' said Spit grumpily.

Alex turned to him. 'Look,' he said, 'this isn't personal. You did it your way, now I'm doing it my way. We may have our differences, but you're part of this team. And we need you.'

'Oh, really,' said Spit, not sounding convinced.

'Really,' said Alex. 'You may get grumpier than any of us, but you're still *one* of us. And that's what counts. You see stuff that the rest of us miss.'

Spit looked at Alex as if he couldn't quite believe what he was hearing. 'What are you saying?'

'I'm saying that we can't do this without you. We need you to stop us from getting carried away and doing something really silly. Your quick thinking has saved our bacon in the past, and you'll probably do it again in the future.'

'He's right,' said Cherry, and House and Inchy nodded their agreement.

'I suppose,' said Spit reluctantly.

'I *know*,' replied Alex with a smile. 'So why don't you start by finding all the torches you can, and plenty of spare batteries. Cherry, you get your bow – it might be useful if we have to fight. Inchy, it could be a maze down there in those tunnels; we're going to need something that will stop us getting lost. I'll dig out my Lucky Dip, and House, you sort out some rations. Let's go!'

Before anyone could move, though, a loud squeak burst from the cage of Gerald the rat.

'What's up with him?' wondered Cherry.

Gerald certainly seemed agitated. He was standing up at the side of his cage, leaning on the bars and squeaking urgently. Most strangely of all, he seemed to be waving to them with his left paw.

'I think he wants to come with us,' said Alex in amazement.

'No way,' said Inchy, slamming his hand down on his bedside table. 'Chasing giant rats down a dark, scary tunnel is one thing, but having one hitch a ride is another thing entirely.'

'But he might be useful,' suggested Alex. 'He might be able to sniff out his ratty friends.'

'If he goes, I stay,' said Inchy flatly, sitting down on his bed and folding his arms.

'He's just a rat,' wheedled Cherry.

'And I'm just an angel,' said Inchy. 'And I need to be alert and not distracted. Knowing Gerald's right beside me will put me off.'

'You're serious, aren't you?' asked Alex.

Inchy nodded.

'OK,' said Alex reluctantly. 'Then Gerald stays. It's probably safer for him here, anyway.'

Inchy breathed a sigh of relief.

'Come on then, team,' Alex said. 'Let's get going.'

'Ow!' said House.

'Watch it, House,' said Spit.

'Er, that was me,' said Alex.

'Where's Inchy?' said Cherry.

'Keeping out of everyone's way,' said Inchy.

It had been surprisingly easy for the gang to

sneak back into the school grounds under cover of darkness and make their way over to the hole that had tried to eat House earlier in the day. Letting down a rope, the five angels had slid down into the yawning chasm in the football pitch and slipped into the tunnel at the bottom.

The passage was surprisingly tall and wide. The team didn't have to stoop to walk through it, and the edges, although straggly with the roots of bushes and trees, were quite smooth. Unfortunately, what the tunnel also was was very long. In fact, even the light of the torch didn't extend far enough to escape the horrible feeling of heading straight into the unknown.

They'd been going for a few hundred metres, when Spit stopped.

'This stinks,' he said.

'Come off it, Spit,' grumbled Cherry. 'I thought we'd agreed that you weren't going to complain all the time.'

'No, I mean it *really* stinks,' replied Spit. 'Can't you smell it?'

The gang sniffed the air.

'Ugh!' grimaced House. 'What is it?'

'School dinners?' suggested Cherry.

'Tabbris's aftershave?' offered Inchy.

'No,' said Alex. 'Drains.'

'Didn't you say that the Skitterlings smelled like drains, Alex?' asked House nervously.

'Yup,' Alex said as the gang moved forward, somewhat more hesitantly than before. 'It's getting stronger too. The tunnel turns right up there. Maybe there's something round the bend.'

'This whole trip's round the bend,' muttered Spit. 'This torch is only minutes away from dying, and we'll probably be close behind.'

The gang crept up to the corner.

'It's really strong now,' whispered Inchy. 'It's making my eyes water.'

'I think I'm gonna be sick.' Even by torchlight, Cherry was an impressive shade of green.

'We can't turn back now,' said Alex, his hand over his mouth and nose to block out the pong. 'Come on. One, two, *three*!'

The gang swung round the corner.

'Blimey,' said House. 'I wasn't expecting that.'

The rough, earthy passage had emerged into a

much larger tunnel. This one was lined with red bricks, covered with thick, green moss. Where the floor should have been, there was just a slow-moving stream of dark, stinking liquid.

'Oh, brilliant,' said Spit. 'Just perfect. I led us to the brink of footie glory, Alex leads us to a river of poo.'

'It's a sewer,' breathed Inchy.

'Yes, I think we'd already worked that out for ourselves,' said Cherry. 'What now?'

'We turn back, of course,' said Spit.

'Hang on,' hissed Alex, raising his hand. 'What's that?'

House looked confused. 'It's the smell of –'

'Not *that*,' said Alex. 'There on the wall. Look!'

The gang looked to where Alex was pointing.

'Scratches,' said Inchy, staring at the deep gouges in the brickwork. 'They look like they were made by claws.'

'But they're huge!' said Cherry.

'Exactly,' replied Alex. 'It *must* be the Skitterlings. And can anyone else hear something?'

The gang fell silent. For a moment, no one could

hear anything except the sound of their own heartbeats, and the water running through the sewer. But then, they all heard it. A faint sound that definitely didn't belong there. A clanking, creaking, mechanical noise, like an old steam train with a really bad case of rheumatism.

'Sounds like cogs and stuff,' whispered Inchy. 'Some sort of machine. What on Earth can it be, down here?'

'The Skitterlings in the kitchen mentioned an engine, remember?' Alex's eyes gleamed triumphantly. 'That's what they were stealing the food for. We're getting close, guys! Come on!'

Alex turned to go.

'Wait!' Spit's voice was low, but urgent. 'Don't you think this is all just a bit too easy? We've come down this tunnel – there have been no barriers, no guards. It could be a trap.'

'A trap,' scoffed Alex. 'I don't think so. The Skitterlings may be sneaky thieves, but –'

Before Alex could finish, a massive shadow leapt from a hole in the side of the sewer wall and grabbed hold of him.

'It's a Skitterling!' cried Inchy.

'Not just one,' yelled Spit. 'Look!'

As if by magic, a whole mob of the weird creatures poured out of the hole.

Without hesitation, House hurled himself forward. He piled into the Skitterlings, tumbling them backwards like dominoes, but there were too many of them. Some were already past him and homing in on the rest of the gang.

Cherry lifted her bow and took aim, but the Skitterlings were too close. One of them reached up and pulled the weapon from her hands, its pointed face grinning horribly.

Alex was still fighting with the first Skitterling, its heavy body pinning him down. Alex thrashed desperately. Maybe something in the Lucky Dip could help him. Tugging the bag out of his pocket, Alex reached for the opening. But the Skitterling got there first. With a squeak of anger, it pulled the Lucky Dip from Alex's hand and threw it across the sewer.

'Oi!' hollered Alex. 'That's mine!' Elbowing the Skitterling sharply in the stomach, he succeeded in knocking the stinking monster off him.

Spit was so busy trying to keep the light of the torch focused so that Alex and House could see what they were doing, he didn't notice the large Skitterling sneaking up behind him.

'Spit!' screamed Inchy, but he was too late. With a swing of its paw, the monster knocked the torch from Spit's hand and into the filthy water, where it spluttered and died, plunging the sewer into darkness.

Chaos filled the tunnel. In the pitch black it was impossible for the gang to tell friend from foe.

'Back up!' yelled Alex. 'Try to get back to the first tunnel! And stick together!'

Ducking and weaving to avoid the hairy arms of the Skitterlings, Alex, Spit, Cherry and Inchy fell back down the passage.

Only House didn't seem willing to retreat. As a Guardian Angel he was trained to fight in all conditions and, even in the darkness, he was holding his own. He waded forward, sending Skitterling after Skitterling flying before him. The rat men were strong, but not a patch on an angry angel who didn't take kindly to creatures that stole food from the school canteen.

Eventually, the Skitterlings started to back off. Their attacks decreased in ferocity until at last House was left alone. He was exhausted, but triumphant – he'd seen the monsters off! He'd won!

'Alex!' he called. 'The Skitterlings are gone!'

The sewer tunnel was strangely quiet.

'Alex?' said House. 'Did you hear me? We're OK now – they've gone!'

No answer.

'Alex?' said House, starting to feel rather alone. 'What's going on? Why aren't you answering?'

Still nothing.

'Spit? Cherry? Inchy?'

A tiny niggling worry began to creep into the back of House's mind. Where could the others be? He couldn't have gone *that* far, surely? He remembered charging forward to attack. Then veering left to avoid a couple of Skitterlings. Then taking another turn. But was it left, or right?

'Oh dear,' muttered House to himself. 'I think I might be lost.'

★ ★ ★

'It's OK,' whispered Alex, his voice barely more than a breath. 'I think they've gone.'

'But gone where?' asked Cherry equally quietly.

'Does it matter?' Spit sounded utterly dejected. 'We've got no way of finding our way out of here without light.'

'Spit's right,' Inchy added. 'We could wander around down here for days.'

'The important thing is not to panic,' said Alex reassuringly. 'We're all safe and that's what matters most. Right, House? House?'

House crept forward, his arms outstretched. He couldn't see a thing. Stinking water sloshed around his feet. Suddenly, his straining eyes spotted a glimmer of light up ahead.

'Thank goodness,' he murmured. 'Maybe it's a manhole cover or something. I'll get out, go and find Tabbris and we'll come back and get the others.'

He slogged on some more. The glimmer of light had been joined by several more glimmers. That was strange. They looked almost like eyes. Little beady eyes . . .

'Uh-oh. Alex –'

Before House could finish his desperate cry, his voice was choked off by a huge, hairy arm that grabbed him from behind. He struggled, but it was no use – dozens of other paws were already grabbing hold of him. There were too many of them.

'Alex! They've got me!' he bellowed. 'Get out and save yourselves! Get out!'

In a distant tunnel, the gang listened in horror as House's cries echoed through the darkness. Their friend was a prisoner of the Skitterlings – and there was nothing they could do about it.

13
A Black Situation

'Impossible!' said Spit. 'I know I don't always see eye to eye with that great lump of an angel, but I don't see how anything could beat him in a fight – not even a gang of rat men.'

'We've got to find him,' said Cherry.

'In this darkness?' replied Alex. 'How? We don't even know where *we* are, never mind where they've taken House! The only way out of this is to use our brains.'

'Then we're truly doomed,' muttered Spit.

'Listen!' said Inchy.

Everyone fell silent. The distant clank of machinery rattled through the tunnel again.

'Look,' said Inchy. 'That noise has to be the mysterious "engine" that Alex heard the Skitterlings talking about. That's why they were stealing the food and I'll bet my wings that it's where they've taken House.'

'You're probably right,' said Alex. 'But can you tell which direction the noise is coming from? I can't.'

Inchy listened carefully, but Alex was right. The echo in the tunnel made it impossible to tell whether the noise was coming from in front of them or behind.

'Anyone got any bright ideas?' asked Alex.

'What about your Lucky Dip?' asked Spit. 'It's got us into trouble plenty of times. Surely it's got something inside to get us out of trouble as well?'

'Oh, it does,' said Alex. 'But the Skitterlings nicked it.'

'Pants,' said Cherry.

'Mega-pants,' corrected Alex.

A faint squeak cut through the noise of distant machinery.

'What was that?' said Spit.

'It's a rat!' flapped Inchy. 'A rat in the dark!'

'Calm down,' said Cherry.

'I can't!' squealed Inchy. 'They're bad enough when I can see them, but when I can't? That's a total nightmare!'

The squeak came again, only closer. This time it sounded as if it was right at their feet.

'Argh!' yelled Inchy. 'It *is* a rat! It's crawling up my leg! It's going to chew my head off and feast on my brains, I know it!'

'Actually, it's on *my* leg,' said Alex. 'And I recognize that squeak.'

'Oh, really?' said Cherry doubtfully. 'Some sort of Doctor Doolittle now, are you?'

Alex felt fur against his cheek as the rat crawled up and sat down on his shoulder. It squeaked once again and nuzzled his cheek affectionately.

'It's Gerald!' whooped Alex.

'Not exactly the cavalry,' muttered Spit.

'He must've followed us from the house,' said

Cherry. 'The clever little thing escaped from his cage!'

'Perhaps he can help us,' said Alex. Before Inchy had a chance to pooh-pooh the idea, he turned to Gerald. 'Look,' he said, 'I know you're a rat and that you probably haven't a clue what I'm saying, but we need your help, OK?'

Gerald squeaked twice. Then he leapt off Alex's shoulder to the ground and scuttled off into the dark.

'He's abandoning us!' Cherry's voice sounded stricken.

'Can't blame him, really,' said Spit.

Then they all heard Gerald scuttling back, more slowly this time.

Alex crouched down and felt carefully around. Finally, his fingers brushed fur.

'He's got something in his mouth,' exclaimed Alex.

'What is it?' said Spit.

There was a sharp click and light flooded the tunnel. The gang threw up their hands to shield their eyes from the dazzling glare. When their eyes had adjusted they saw Alex grinning like a loon. In one hand was a small, portable torch. In the other . . .

'My Lucky Dip,' crowed Alex. 'And our spare torch was in it too – Gerald must have known it was just what we needed!'

'That's one clever rat,' remarked Cherry.

'Maybe Roddan's chocolate was designed to make them brainier as well as brawnier,' said Inchy thoughtfully.

'Now, let's see if we can't find House,' suggested Alex.

'Good plan,' agreed Cherry.

With Alex taking the lead and Gerald happily riding on his shoulder, the gang shuffled off into the dark. The tunnel wound on and on, seeming to have no end, the distant thrum of machinery gradually getting louder and louder. Finally, after what seemed like an age, the tunnel split, giving them a choice of directions.

Alex paused. It was impossible to tell from which tunnel the engine sound was coming.

'Which way now?' asked Spit.

'Haven't a clue,' said Alex. 'You?'

'No idea,' said Spit.

'Great,' snapped Cherry. 'Now what?'

With a squeak, Gerald leapt off Alex's shoulder. Running up to the left-hand passage, he sat up on his hind legs and sniffed the air. Then he scuttled over to the right-hand tunnel and did the same. For a moment, the little rat sat quite still, almost as if he was thinking. Then, with a twitch of his whiskers, he dived down the right-hand route.

'Gerald knows the way!' laughed Alex. 'He can smell the others! Come on!'

'I can't believe we're following a rat,' said Inchy.

'Bet you're glad I rescued him from the classroom now, eh?' chortled Alex as the others fell in behind him.

The tunnel wound its way on through the earth. The gang prowled carefully, keeping their eyes and ears open for the tell-tale signs of Skitterlings, but there was no sign of the furry monsters. Finally, Alex stopped.

'There's a light up ahead,' he pointed out.

It was true. A faint gleam shone from beyond the

next bend in the tunnel. The clanking and grinding of metal on metal was louder than ever.

'I think we're almost there. Be careful . . .'

Alex led the way as the team crept forward and peered round the corner.

From the shadows of the tunnel, they stared out into an enormous brick-built chamber. The roof towered above them, arched and dark, the very top of it hidden in shadow. Around the edges of the room, clanking and whirring and spinning, was a series of metal wheels. They looked just like the kind of wheels that rats, mice or hamsters would run in to exercise. Except that these wheels were at least four metres in diameter, and the rats running round and round inside them were the size of wolves. Standing next to each wheel was a Skitterling. The evil-looking rat men were each holding a leather whip. If any of the rats looked like they were slowing down, the Skitterling would lash them cruelly.

'Look,' hissed Inchy, pointing. 'The wheels must be powering that machine over there.'

'What *is* it?' asked Cherry.

No one had an answer. The machine stood in the very centre of the room, an impossible tangle of twisting pipes, tubes and cogs. It was connected to each of the giant wheels by a cat's cradle of wires and cables that sparked with the electricity being generated by the running rats. And at the very centre of the machine was a large glass globe filled with a horrible, gloopy liquid that bubbled and steamed, glowing a sickly shade of green.

'Oh no . . .' groaned Alex.

'That doesn't sound encouraging,' sighed Cherry.

'Look at that green stuff,' he said. 'It's got all kinds of muck and rubbish floating about in it. Even dead rats. But that's not the worst of it.'

'What do you mean?' demanded Spit.

'Can't you see?' said Alex. 'Under there.'

The rest of the gang followed his pointing finger. And saw House.

Their big friend was tightly strapped to something that resembled an old shopping trolley that had been rescued from a canal. But what was even more surprising was the sight of the person standing over House, tinkering with the machine.

'Mr Roddan!' Spit whistled. 'He's not dead!'

'No, he's not,' agreed Alex. 'And by the look of him, he's not human, either.'

It was true. Their former science teacher had changed beyond all recognition. His body was covered with patchy fur. Where his skin showed through, it was red and flaky, as if he'd been scratching it too much. His movements were even more rat-like than normal – nervous and jerky. Worst of all, from the back of his tattered trousers protruded a stubby little tail that lashed to and fro as he moved.

'How stupid are we?' said Cherry, slapping her forehead with her palm. 'We thought that the rats had eaten Roddan – but instead he's working with them!'

A harsh laugh echoed round the chamber. Whatever Mr Roddan was doing, he was clearly enjoying it.

'Comfortable are we, boy?' he croaked, staring down at House.

'Not really,' said House. 'And you'd better let me go right now, or there'll be trouble.'

'Oh, scary,' laughed Roddan. 'You think I fear you, boy? That I'm scared? You are a fool!'

'Maybe, but I'm not the one who's turned himself into a giant rat,' sniffed House.

'I'm not a giant rat,' shouted Roddan, bristling. 'I am becoming a Skitterling. I have all the strength and intelligence of a human, plus the speed and cunning of a rat!'

'I'm pleased for you,' said House. 'Let's see how much good your cunning does you when I smash up your precious machine and punch your silly, twitchy nose in.'

'Stupid child! Do you really think that you are in any position to damage my Plague Engine?' Roddan collapsed in a fit of hysterical laughter.

'He's really playing up the whole insane villain thing, isn't he?' said Spit.

'A Plague Engine?' said Inchy. 'That doesn't sound good . . .'

Roddan's laugh ended in a horrible, phlegmy cough and he spat a gob of mucus on to the floor.

He continued with his speech. 'The Skitterlings have worked well for me. Stealing food from the town to feed my rats!'

'They're the ones from our class, aren't they?' said

House. 'You put something in the chocolate that made them grow bigger. Why?'

'Why?' replied Roddan. 'Why? Look around you, boy. My Plague Engine needs power – power provided by those wheels over there. But normal rats are just too small. So I had to make them bigger – now they provide me with all the power I need!'

'But what do you need power for?' demanded House. 'What are you going to do?'

Mr Roddan laughed again. 'Why, I'm going to kill everyone in Green Hill, of course.'

'Kill everyone?' House spluttered. 'You can't!'

'Ah, but I can, boy,' said Roddan. 'You see that green stuff bubbling away there?' He pointed at the glass globe at the heart of the machine. 'That's another one of my most brilliant inventions – liquid plague!'

'Liquid plague?' Inchy's voice was disbelieving. 'That's horrible!'

'It's been brewing away for weeks now, and it's almost ready. When it's finished, all I need to do is to inject it into the Green Hill water supply and it will infect everyone in this miserable town. From there the plague will spread all over the globe. It will be a new Black Death! And then the world will belong to me!'

'He's serious, isn't he?' said Cherry.

'Unfortunately, it looks that way,' replied Alex.

House stared at Mr Roddan, his face a mask of horror. 'What are you going to do with me?'

'Well, I have to make absolutely sure that my plague is ready, don't I?' he gurgled. 'And that means I need to test it. Your human scientists do all their testing on animals, you know. Lab rats. But I don't have any rats to spare. So I'll have to use something else.'

Roddan leaned over him and House nearly gagged at his reeking breath.

'You.'

14
Highly Strung

House glared back into Mr Roddan's mad eyes. Deep down he was a little scared, but he wasn't about to let that show. He was an angel – and a Guardian Angel at that. He wasn't about to give ratty Roddan the satisfaction of seeing him afraid, no matter what. Besides, he knew that his only chance was to keep Roddan talking. That might buy Alex and the others enough time to find him and work out some way of preventing the wacky teacher's murderous plan.

'But what's in it for you?' he demanded, struggling against the ropes that had him tied down.

'What's in it for me?' repeated Roddan. 'More than you can imagine, child. I have communed with powers deep and dark,' he hissed. 'Powers that have promised me the Earth!'

Roddan cackled madly.

House felt his blood run cold. At first, he'd thought that Roddan was just insane — a mad scientist acting alone. But something about the words he had used suggested something else. *Powers deep and dark* . . . The thought made House shudder.

'What powers?' he asked. 'What have you done, Roddan?'

'Demons!' yelled Roddan, flicking round. 'Demons, boy, that's what powers! When all you humans are dead, their Master has promised me that my Skitterlings shall inherit the Earth!'

Far off in the shadows at the edge of the chamber the gang gasped.

'Not again,' groaned Cherry. 'What is it with demons and Green Hill?'

'Never mind that, we've got to stop him,' said Inchy.

'I say we just get in there and kick his skinny backside into the middle of next week,' said Cherry. 'Who's with me?'

Alex shook his head. 'There are too many Skitterlings,' he said. 'And without your bow, we stand even less of a chance.'

'We've got no choice!' said Cherry. 'House needs us!'

'We're running out of time!' exclaimed Inchy. 'Look!'

Roddan had turned his back on House and was now standing at what looked like the control panel for his Plague Engine. As he pulled levers and pushed switches, the machine began to respond, letting out a low hum, like an organ warming up in a cathedral.

'That's totally weird,' said Spit. 'The machine is designed to wipe out all human life, but it sounds like it's playing music.'

Alex looked up at Spit, his eyes bulging. 'That's it!' he said. 'You're a genius!'

'What's it?' asked Spit, confused, but Alex was too busy rummaging around in his Lucky Dip to answer.

'Here it is,' he said, pulling out a miniature harp. 'Inchy, you remember how you used your music to charm Gerald?'

Inchy nodded.

'Reckon you can make it work on those giant rats as well? If you can stop them running round those wheels, Roddan's engine will be out of power.'

Spit choked. 'Are you serious? What do you think he is, the Pied Piper?'

'Got any better ideas?' snapped Alex. 'No? Didn't think so! Inchy?'

Inchy shrugged. 'Well, it can't hurt to try, can it?' With that, he put his fingers to the harp.

Inchy's tune was all low notes and faint, high trills. It sounded like wind blowing through a wood on an autumn afternoon, the notes rising and falling, gentle and tuneful.

'It's not working,' said Spit, folding his arms. 'The rats aren't interested. Except Mr Roddan – he's interested all right.'

Alex turned to look. The sound of the music had drawn Roddan's attention. He was staring over at the gang, his eyes full of murderous intent.

'I think he's seen us,' Cherry gulped.

'Doesn't matter!' whooped Alex. 'Look!'

On Alex's shoulder, Gerald was fast asleep.

'And look at the others!'

It was almost unbelievable, but the giant rats racing round in the generator-wheels were slowing down. One or two of the smaller ones were already curling up at the bottom of their wheels. The drone of the Plague Engine was already sounding quieter.

'Stop them! Get them!' shrieked Roddan, gesturing wildly towards the gang. The whip-bearing Skitterlings tried to respond, but it was clear that Inchy's tune seemed to be affecting them too. The rat men stumbled towards the gang as if they were drunk, rubbing their eyes and yawning.

'I think now's our best chance to get House,' said Alex.

'But the Skitterlings aren't fully asleep,' objected Cherry.

'That's a risk I'll have to take,' said Alex and

165

before anyone could stop him he was off, racing across the chamber towards House.

'Always being the hero,' said Spit.

'At least he's good at it,' Cherry shot back.

'Oh yeah?' snapped Spit, bristling. 'Watch this!'

And with that, he raced out into the chamber himself.

'Hey! Rat features!' he yelled at the Skitterlings who were staggering over to block Alex's way. 'Come on! Over here!'

The Skitterlings looked at Alex, then at Spit, then back to Alex again.

'I said over here, cheese-breath!' taunted Spit. 'Your mother was a mouse!'

Hissing angrily, the Skitterlings turned away from Alex, and stumbled towards Spit.

'Inchy, keep playing! Alex, get House!' shouted Spit, letting the Skitterlings close in on him before turning to run in the opposite direction, blowing raspberries behind him. It was the perfect distraction – the rat men were completely ignoring Alex. He had a clear path to House.

Alex didn't wait another second. He dashed over

to his friend and quickly untied the straps holding him down.

'Thanks, mate,' grinned House. 'You're a sight for sore eyes.'

The musical hum from the Plague Engine had all but disappeared now. The only noise in the chamber was Inchy's sleepy harp tune and the sound of gentle snoring – every one of the giant rats was asleep. There was no power left in the machine at all. Mr Roddan stood at the control panel angrily stabbing buttons and squeaking out swear words at the top of his voice.

'Come on,' said Alex. 'Let's get out of here.'

Scooping up Cherry's bow, which the Skitterlings had stashed beneath the shopping trolley, the two angels ran back to Cherry and Inchy, arriving at the same time as an out-of-breath Spit. The Skitterlings who had been chasing him crawled slowly after him on all fours, hardly able to keep their eyes open.

'Good work, Spit,' grinned Alex. 'Now we only have to destroy that Plague Engine. And before anyone groans, I have a plan. You know how the slow music made the rats slow down and fall asleep?'

The gang nodded in unison.

'Well, I'd bet anything that, if Inchy played something really fast, they'd wake up and get faster.'

'What would that do?' asked Spit.

'If they speed up, then they'll turn the wheels faster, won't they?' replied Alex. 'And if they do that, Roddan's horrible machine will overload.'

'Are you sure?' asked Cherry.

'Not exactly,' grimaced Alex.

'But it's a good gamble,' said Inchy.

And with that, he changed the tune. Suddenly, the music became like a storm blowing hard through a mountain range, a gale capable of ripping trees from the ground. Faster and faster Inchy played, his fingers flying over the strings of his harp.

'It's working!' said Cherry. 'The rats are going nuts!'

It was true. Waking up from their slumber, the giant rats were racing round inside their wheels. Sparks were already beginning to crackle down the wires that connected the wheels to the Plague Engine, as the rodents ran faster and faster.

'And look at the Skitterlings!' laughed House,

pointing as the rat men started jogging – then sprinting – around the chamber. As the gang watched, two Skitterlings met in a head-on collision that sent both of them sprawling.

'Roddan's not happy,' said Spit.

Everyone turned to look at the mad teacher. He was standing *on top* of his control panel now, bouncing up and down, screaming and pulling his whiskers.

'Stop it! Stop it!' he squeaked. 'Too much power! Too much power!'

The Plague Engine was shaking now. Flashes of electricity raced across the tangled mesh of pipes and pistons.

'I think now would be a good time to duck,' said Alex.

The gang nodded, dropping to their knees.

And with a thunderous roar, the Plague Engine exploded.

15
The Rat's Whiskers

'I've never been so glad of a hot shower and a clean T-shirt in my whole life,' sighed Inchy, sinking back against his pillows.

'All in all, another successful mission,' smiled Alex.

'Except that all the evidence was buried under tons of earth at the bottom of a sewer,' remarked Spit. 'So once again we don't get any credit.'

After the Plague Engine had exploded, the gang had quickly made their way back to the surface, led by Gerald, who seemed to have an unerring instinct for the quickest way home.

'Who would have thought that Mr Roddan was working with demons?' mused Cherry.

'Do you think he really was?' asked House. 'Or was he just a loony?'

'Probably a bit of both,' replied Alex. 'You'd have to be mad to want to change yourself into a rat, but only a demon could convince someone that destroying the world with the plague was a good idea.'

'Well, it was certainly an original plan,' said Inchy. 'Using germs as a weapon is a lot sneakier than zombies.'

'The trouble with Roddan,' said Spit, 'is that he let power go to his head.'

'How's that?' asked Alex, raising an eyebrow.

'Well, he wasn't happy with just controlling the Skitterlings, was he? He could have been King of Rat-land, but he went too far and decided he wanted the whole world. Power crazy!'

'Something you'd know nothing about, of course,' laughed Inchy.

'Well, I did get a bit carried away, I admit. But it was only because I wanted to get us back to Heaven!'

'No one's denying that your heart's in the right place,' said Alex.

'It's just your brain that isn't,' Cherry added.

Everyone laughed.

'Being a leader isn't easy,' said Spit. 'Is it, Alex?'

'Not really. But then I didn't realize how hard it was to be one of the team if the leader doesn't listen to what you've got to say. I think I'll be better at listening now I know what it's like from the other side.'

Inchy looked over at Spit and Alex. 'You know, I think I've worked it out.'

'Worked what out?' said Alex.

'Why you two argue so much.'

'Oh, I can't wait to hear this,' said Spit.

'It's because you're so alike,' finished Inchy triumphantly.

Spit and Alex both looked so shocked by this revelation that House and Cherry burst into laughter.

'It's *so* true!' gasped Cherry.

'He has got a point,' said House.

For a moment it looked like Alex and Spit were about to argue. Then Alex held out his hand. Spit shook it.

Then a roar of fury shook the building, followed by the thunder of limping footsteps and Tabbris burst into the room.

Their guardian was clutching Inchy's T-shirt and Alex's pants, both of which were still dripping black, stinking liquid.

'What on Earth have you been doing this time?' he bellowed. 'And what have you done to my nice, new, *clean* bathroom? It looks like a manure heap has exploded in there!'

'Well, not exactly –' started Alex, but Tabbris was in full flow.

'What happened to setting an example, Respite? How could you have let this happen?'

'But it wasn't –' began Spit.

'And how could *I* have been so foolish as to think that you . . . you . . . you *hooligans* could possibly change your ways?'

'That's a bit harsh, isn't –'

'I am going to speak to Gabriel *this minute*, and you five will be on triple chores for a month! I'll have you . . .'

Tabbris's voice trailed off. His face went as white as his moustache, which was trembling. He looked as if he was having a heart attack. His watery eyes bulged, as if they wanted to pop out of his head and run off down the landing. His gaze was fixed on Alex's bed.

The gang turned to see what he was looking at.

There on the pillow, calmly cleaning his whiskers, sat Gerald.

'Oh no!' moaned House.

'I can explain,' said Inchy in a desperate rush. 'That's Gerald. He came from school. And our teacher wanted to feed him this weird growth potion that would turn him into a super-rat. But Alex rescued him and brought him back here. But he's not dirty or anything – I used to think rats were filthy creatures, but then Gerald saved us when we were lost in the sewers and I realized that they're actually clever and pretty cool. And you're not listening to me at all, are you?'

Tabbris's frozen face twitched.

'It's a r— A r— A *rat*!'

With a bloodcurdling shriek, Tabbris turned and bolted from the room. The gang heard his cry of terror all the way down the stairs, through the front door and down the garden path.

'Well, well, well,' grinned Inchy. 'Who would've thought that a retired angelic war hero would be afraid of rats? Makes me feel a bit better!'

'Enjoy it while you can,' replied Cherry. 'He'll have us on *quadruple* chores soon enough, eh, Alex?'

But Alex wasn't listening. He was staring through the open door in disbelief. This changed everything. At last there was a chink in Tabbris's armour . . .

Alex turned to the gang.

'So,' he said, a wicked smile spreading across his face. 'Who votes we get down to the pet shop and buy a few friends for Gerald . . .?'

There's trouble brewing
down on Earth . . .
And they've landed right in it!

Get your claws into
Demon Defenders!

puffin.co.uk

Who knew that Earth could be so much fun?

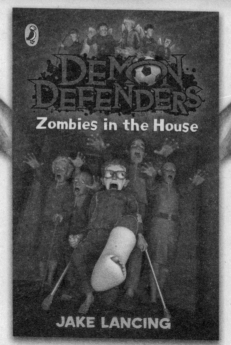

Get your claws into Demon Defenders!

puffin.co.uk

Alex, Spit, House, Inchy and Cherry – a footie team with a difference!

Look out for Goblin Games COMING SOON!

Get your claws into Demon Defenders!

puffin.co.uk

Illustration by Andy Parker

It all started with a Scarecrow

Puffin is well over sixty years old.
Sounds ancient, doesn't it? But Puffin has never been
so lively. We're always on the lookout for the next big
idea, which is how it began all those years ago.

Penguin Books was a big idea from the mind of
a man called Allen Lane, who in 1935 invented
the quality paperback and changed the world.
**And from great Penguins, great Puffins grew,
changing the face of children's books forever.**

The first four Puffin Picture Books were hatched in 1940 and the
first Puffin story book featured a man with broomstick arms called
Worzel Gummidge. In 1967 Kaye Webb, Puffin Editor, started the
Puffin Club, promising to **'make children into readers'**.
She kept that promise and over 200,000 children became
devoted Puffineers through their quarterly instalments of
Puffin Post, which is now back for a new generation.

Many years from now, we hope you'll look back and
remember Puffin with a smile. **No matter what your age
or what you're into, there's a Puffin for everyone.**
The possibilities are endless, but one thing is for sure:
whether it's a picture book or a paperback, a sticker book
or a hardback, **if it's got that little Puffin
on it – it's bound to be good.**